MR. AUGUST

HEROES OF ROGUE VALLEY: CALENDAR GUYS
BOOK 8

ANN ROTH

OLIVERHEIN BOOKS

Copyright © 2018 Ann Roth

Published by Oliver-Heber Books

0 9 8 7 6 5 4 3 2 1

 Created with Vellum

INTRODUCTION

Welcome to Ann Roth's exciting new series, Heroes of Rogue Valley: Calendar Guys series. *Twelve months, 12 gorgeous firefighter heroes and the women who steal into their hearts and forever change their lives.*

Meet Mr. August:

Twice divorced firefighter Nate Gorton is ready to settle down for good—if only he understood women better. After several failed relationships, Becca Chambers has decided to stay single. In high school, Nate had a crush on Becca but she barely noticed him. They haven't seen each other since. Now they're in a wedding together. Nate is still drawn to her and she's still uninterested, but she agrees to teach him what a woman really wants. Nate takes Becca's advice to heart. Suddenly she's changing her mind about him. Will the past prevent them from finding the happiness they both deserve?

Mr. August—Nate Horton
    Age 34, 6'2" tall, 187 pounds
    Single
    Proud Senior Firefighter
    Time with Guff's Lake Fire Department: 13 years

1

What with responding to email queries, evaluating the items people wanted to sell, and running Second Hand Rose six days a week, Becca Chambers barely had time to eat lunch, let alone view personal email during the day. But thanks to the brutal July heat, business had slowed considerably.

Also, the subject line of a personal email snagged her attention like a three-hundred-dollar dresser offered for fifty.

Charlie and Scarlett's Wedding—important reminder!

How could Becca resist that? It wasn't every day her best friend and her brother married each other. She was thrilled for them. And also a little envious, which was odd, considering she didn't want to get married. Not anymore. She'd made her peace with being single and enjoyed living life on her own terms. Although she could do without the intense pangs of loneliness that occasionally struck. She felt one now.

Never mind, it would pass. Marissa, one of the bridesmaids and the self-appointed point person of the group, had sent the email. Becca read it.

Seven weeks and counting until the big day! Bridal shower in one month! As bridesmaids and groomsmen, we have decisions to make. See you at Lucky Joe's tonight at 7:00.

The meeting date had been set weeks ago, and was on Becca's calendar. She looked forward to planning the bridal shower and talking about the dresses Scarlett had picked out for her and the two other women in the wedding.

She'd intended to leave work mid-afternoon, then head home and eat leftovers for dinner. But having sent Petal, her assistant, home for the day, Becca no longer had that option. Good thing the shop closed early on weekdays during summer.

She scanned the list of recipients. Six people including herself and the best man, all of whom she knew. Not uncommon in Guff's Lake.

Charlie had chosen Nate Horton as his best man. They'd been friends since high school and ran a business together—Charlie full time, and Nate when he wasn't doing his thing at the Guff's Lake Fire Department.

Becca hadn't seen Nate in ages, but who could forget how amazing he looked in a tux on prom night? She'd had a secret crush on him forever.

Meanwhile, he'd had a number of girlfriends and two wives.

The mere thought of all those breakups, all that upheaval, made her cringe. She preferred, no insisted on, calm and balance in her life.

Back to dinner. She had to eat something before the meeting. Why not at Lucky Joe's? Problem solved.

The bell over the door tinkled and a young couple wandered in. Greeting them with a welcoming smile, Becca went to work.

As a rule, Nate Horton preferred physical activity to sitting on his ass. After doing exactly that for hours while he and Charlie fine-tuned the details for the privately owned Bombardier Learjet their new client wanted them to upgrade to top-of-the-line, Nate itched to get outside and do something physical.

Courtesy of the setting sun and mild breeze that lowered the blistering temperature a good fifteen degrees, this was a perfect evening for a bike ride in the foothills of the Siskiyou Mountains, followed by a cold beer and a hearty meal. Nothing better.

Instead, here he was, ambling toward the entrance to Lucky Joe's for a pre-wedding meeting. Not his idea of fun.

Who wanted to sit around several more

hours, hashing over details of a wedding that wasn't for another seven weeks? Hell, he'd already ordered his tux and marked the rehearsal dinner and the date and time of the wedding on his calendar. He'd also thought up several ideas for the bachelor party. What else was there to do?

On the upside, he'd see Becca. It'd been a while. He'd had a thing for her since Charlie introduced them way back when, but she'd never given him the time of day. Probably for the best, as she was a class act, and he was a regular guy who happened to suck at romance.

He checked his watch. Forty-five minutes until the meeting—time enough to grab dinner.

The live music Lucky Joe's offered Friday and Saturday nights always drew a decent weekend crowd, but on a Thursday night, the club was quiet. Nate had his pick of tables.

He was about to sit down when he spotted Becca near the bar. She was eating alone, bent over a manila folder and scribbling with a pen, her dark brown hair pulled into a loose ponytail and her cute nose wrinkled in concentration.

As always, so far out of his league... Like a tomcat drawn to a shiny, irresistible treasure, he made a beeline for her. "Hey," he said, hesitating a beat before bending down to kiss her cheek.

She didn't seem to mind. Her soft brown eyes almost lit up—a first in his experience. In the past, she'd never looked twice at him.

"Hi, Nate. It's been awhile."

Beautiful and she smelled good. After all these years, he still carried a torch for her. Big waste of time, but there it was.

"Like you, I came early to eat before the meeting," he said. "Mind if I join you? If I'm not interrupting."

"This?" She gestured at a computer printout. "I'm reviewing my inventory and figuring out what I need to stock before fall. I'd much rather catch up. Please, sit down."

Nate took the chair across from her. "Charlie says 'Hi.' I reminded him you'd be here tonight."

"He has other things on his mind."

Becca's brother was wrapped up in Scarlett, and Nate and Becca shared a knowing smile before he signaled the idle waiter lingering nearby.

After he ordered, he really looked at Becca for the first time. When she wasn't smiling or caught up in work, fatigue etched her face. "How have you been?" he asked.

"Busy, although this time of year is slow. The business keeps growing."

"Cool. Same with Charlie's and my private plane business."

Becca's napkin sat on her lap, but she seemed to be finished with her meal. He eyed the untouched cheese potatoes on her plate. "You're not eating those?"

"I need to take off a few pounds before the wedding so I can fit into my dress."

He let his gaze rove over her face and as far

down her body as the table allowed. Creamy shoulders, sleeveless blouse cut in a vee that almost reached her generous breasts... "You look good to me."

She shifted in her seat and dropped her gaze. He'd made her uncomfortable, the last thing he wanted. He nodded at her plate. "So do those potatoes."

"Help yourself."

Nate did. "Man, I'm hungry. Charlie and I spent most of the day working on a new interior for a client who wants the best money can buy."

"I can't imagine what that's like, but it sounds fun."

"It can be. People with that kind of money tend to be finicky and difficult to please. Considering what we charge, the headaches are worth the time and effort. Our challenge with this particular job is to finish it before the wedding."

"Does the client want that, too?" Becca asked.

"He wouldn't mind. It's more Charlie's decision, so that he can focus on getting married."

"I'll cross my fingers. I want this wedding to go off without a hitch, and if you don't finish... You know how distracted Charlie gets when he's working."

"I'm the same way. Don't worry, we'll meet Charlie's deadline. What kind of inventory do you need for the fall?"

"Everything. Furniture, school clothes, dishes, winter coats—"

"For college kids renting apartments," Nate guessed.

"That, too. When the weather is hot like now, people don't shop much. They come back in September."

"I haven't been in Second Hand Rose for years. I could use a lamp, if you have any."

"We have a nice selection of floor and table lamps, and quite a few lava lamps."

"No kidding. I haven't seen one of those since I was a kid."

"They're popular again."

When Becca talked about her shop, her whole face lit up—a real treat.

"Are you seeing anyone right now?" Nate asked. Why had he even bothered? She'd never shown a spark of interest in him.

She shook her head. "By choice."

"Because?"

"Charlie didn't tell you about my last breakup?"

"He said it caught you by surprise."

"More like stunned. Craig had invited me to a nice restaurant to mark the third anniversary of our first date, and I was sure he was going to propose. Instead he broke up with me."

"Ouch."

"That about sums it up."

"I'm pretty battle scarred myself and also single." Two years divorced for the second time, Nate was ready to climb back in the saddle and try again. This time for good. If only he could figure out what women wanted.

Becca would know.

Now, there was an idea...

He was about to propose it when his food arrived. For a while, he focused on filling his belly. When he glanced up from his plate, he caught Becca silently laughing.

"What?" he said.

"I see you're still a bottomless pit."

"Hey, Charlie and I worked through lunch." He pushed his plate aside. "I could use your help."

"*My* help?" She frowned.

Before he could explain, Bryan and Travis, Charlie's groomsmen, called out to him. Seconds later, the two bridesmaids arrived. Three men, three women.

They pushed two tables together, ordered drinks, and got down to business.

"All right, we women need to plan something fun for Scarlett's bridal shower," Marissa announced sometime later. "Why don't you guys plan the bachelor party at a different table?"

Nate and the other two men collected their beer mugs and settled into a booth across the way.

Watching him move was a pleasure. Tall and muscled, he exuded strength and confidence. Catching herself in a dreamy sigh, Becca hastily stuffed her gushy feelings deep inside.

"Scarlett's mom is throwing her a traditional shower," Marissa said. "What do we want to do?"

While they shared ideas, Becca stifled a yawn. As much as she enjoyed planning and socializing, she was tired. The glass of wine she'd drunk with dinner hadn't exactly perked her up.

She hadn't felt at all weary while she and Nate talked. She heard laughter and glanced over at his booth. His head was thrown back in full-fledged mirth. Such an attractive man.

"Did either of you happen to read the article in yesterday's paper about the grand opening for Wanda Lipmann's new day spa at Tommie's Hair and Nails?" she asked. "I think we should spend the day there, getting pampered, and then take Scarlett to dinner."

Marissa and Alexis, the second bridesmaid, loved the suggestion. They set to work divvying up jobs to make the day happen. Alexis offered to get prices and availability both for Wanda's new venture and the spa at Guff's Lake Resort, Marissa agreed to work on transportation—so that they could enjoy their champagne without worrying about driving—and Becca volunteered to find a restaurant.

As the evening wound down, she stole another glance at Nate. And caught him looking straight at her. Even from across the room, she could see his pale green eyes bright and interested. No man had the right to eyes that striking.

Face it, he was far above average in every way. Make that spectacular, from his short-cropped red-brown hair to his rugged features. And those broad shoulders... He needed them to carry the weight of his muscular biceps.

He grinned as if he could read her thoughts. She hastily averted her gaze.

"Nate seems into you," Marissa murmured.

Becca doubted that. "We know each other

from when he and Charlie played football together in high school. They've been good friends
since, and also co-own their plane business, but
Nate and I haven't seen each other in forever. He
wants to catch up, that's all."

He'd also asked for her help. About what? Cu-
riosity ate at her.

"I disagree," Alexis said. "The way he keeps
looking at you? The man is definitely interested.
Would you go out with him?"

Although Becca intended to stay single, she
hadn't ruled out dating. But with Nate, who had
tons of failed relationships under his belt? No
matter how much she liked him and how at-
tracted she was to him, they could never date.
She had no interest in getting mixed up in his
chaotic world. Anyway, her quiet lifestyle would
probably bore him to death. "I don't think so."

Alexis shook her head. "If I weren't serious
with Fritz, I would. I'd invite Nate to have a beer
with me. You're single, he's single, why not?"

In no mood to discuss her dating life, Becca
stretched and yawned. "As much fun as I'm having, it's getting late. I know I'm not the only one
who has to work tomorrow. Let's finish up and go
home."

❧

AFTER SAYING her good-byes and using the
women's bathroom at Lucky Joe's, Becca returned

to the dining area. She didn't expect to find Nate waiting for her.

"You're still here," she said.

"We didn't finish our conversation. Can I buy you another glass of wine?"

"Better not—I'm sleepy enough as it is. I could drink a lemonade, though."

At the bar, Nate ordered two. They sat down at their original table.

"You wanted to ask me something?" she prodded, dying to know.

"Because you're a woman..." He looked her over with unconcealed warmth.

A wave of pleasure washed through her, which she quickly dismissed. "And you're a man. Go on."

"I need tips on how to figure out what women want."

Was he serious? She frowned. "You've had girlfriends and you've been married. You obviously know how."

"It might look that way from the outside. Getting a date is easy, but bottom line? I always pick the wrong woman. Two divorces and more broken relationships than I can count... I'm doing something wrong, but for the life of me, I can't figure out what."

Becca understood, since she was in the same boat. "Not necessarily. Dating is an iffy proposition. Sometimes things go well, other times, not."

"For me, they always go south. Trouble getting

along, lots of fighting... My lousy record speaks for itself."

"I remember when you got married right out of high school. Do you mind telling me what happened?"

"Not at all. She wouldn't have sex without a ring on her finger, so I gave her what she wanted." He snorted. "Pretty lame, huh?"

"You were young and didn't know any better."

"That's what I told myself when it ended. I waited until I was twenty-nine to try again. My second wife had a drinking problem. In the end, she chose the bottle over me."

"That's awful, but it could happen to anyone. Her alcoholism wasn't your fault."

"True. But the signs were there from the beginning, only I refused to see them." He rubbed his hand over his face.

There was something they had in common. Not that Craig was a big drinker, but near the end of their relationship, Becca had noticed he was increasingly withdrawn and restless. Instead of trying to find out what was wrong, she'd ignored her doubts, put on a happy face and pretended everything was wonderful. Part of her MO. For the sake of keeping the peace, she tended to ignore troubling signs, bury frustrations, and keep smiling.

"I'm older and wiser now, and I'm looking for a woman willing to work on the relationship so that it doesn't fail," Nate said. "Is that too much to ask?"

"I don't think so, but I'm no expert. Like you, none of my relationships have worked out, " she admitted. "I'm at the point now that I don't even want to get married."

"Ever?"

"I have a full life, and I'm happy being single." She forced a smile to prove it.

"I've never known a woman to say that."

"Now you have."

"If you did want to get married, what would you want in a man?"

His intent look put her on the spot. Under the table, she crossed and re-crossed her legs. "Why would you want to know that?"

"Because I need all the help I can get."

Not wanting to make this about her, she spoke for all females. "I don't know of a single woman who doesn't want to be heard. We want a man to put us first, yet at the same time treat us as his equal. He should also respect and value our opinions, and be open about his feelings toward us and about us as a couple. Making decisions together would also be nice. No fighting, either."

"Come on, Becca. At times, every couple fights."

She shuddered. "I don't."

His eyes narrowed a fraction. "What did your ex do to you?"

"Nothing except break up with me. Anyway, I don't see what that has to do with your situation."

"I hit a nerve and I want to know why."

"It's not a secret. I'm sure you know from Charlie that throughout our childhood, our parents were always at each other's throats. And I mean constantly. Things got so bad that when I was in high school they almost divorced." Remembering, she winced. "I will never be involved in a relationship like that."

"Who would? No one wants to fight all the time, but people who spend time together are bound to have disagreements. What are they supposed to do then?"

"Have you met Scarlett's parents? They have a one in a million relationship—they're close, caring, and loving toward one another. They never fight."

"Never?"

Nate's obvious skepticism bothered her more than it should have. She squinted at him. "Do you want my help or not?"

"Yeah, but not if it upsets you."

He held up both hands, as if to placate her. Which set off all kinds of mad inside. And was so unlike her. She didn't understand her reaction. Didn't like it, either.

Calm down. Anxious to regain her composure, Becca inhaled through her nose and slowly exhaled through her mouth. *There.*

She managed a tight smile. "I'm not at all upset. FYI, in high school, I spent a lot of time at Scarlett's." A welcome refuge from the tension and screaming at home. "I saw first-hand how her parents dealt with disagreements. They worked out their differences peacefully, through discussions, not arguments."

Since then, she'd dreamed of having a relationship like theirs. No luck, but she was trying to make a point.

Pleased with her solid reasoning and rational tone, she sat back and folded her hands on the table. "I don't fight with men I'm involved with. Period."

"Wow," Nate said. "I've never known any couple in any relationship to not argue from time to time. But as I said, I'm clueless about these things."

Pleased that he'd heard her, Becca nodded. "Maybe you should try the not fighting thing with your girlfriends." She checked her watch, surprised to find an hour had passed since she and Nate had again sat down. "Gosh, it's late. I meant to leave awhile ago."

3

N ate had his doubts about avoiding arguments *all* the time. But for the sake of meeting the right woman, he was determined to keep an open mind.

Plus, he enjoyed being with Becca and wanted to see her again before the wedding—even if she was a cut or three above his ass and totally uninterested in him. He sure as hell was interested in her. So sue him. A guy could try. More than that, he needed her help.

"I'm willing to try anything, but I need coaching and practice," he said as they exited Lucky Joe's and headed toward their cars. The sun had set, but there were plenty of lights in the lot. "Would you be interested in tutoring me?"

Her chin angled upward and she screwed up her mouth, just like when she'd mulled something over in high school. "But I'm an amateur. Surely there are trained experts you could learn more from."

"I want to work with you."

"Hmm. What are you looking to learn?"

At least a dozen problem areas sprang to mind. First and foremost, the one that made the least sense. "I don't understand how to avoid an argument, unless there's a way to stop it before it starts. Can you teach me that?"

"What you're looking for is conflict resolution. I'll do my best."

Couldn't ask for more than that. Nate had planned to play poker the next night with his crewmates at the standing weekly game—show up and join in—but he preferred to spend his evening learning something useful from Becca. "Are you free tomorrow night?"

"You want to spend your Friday night on a lesson?"

"If you're willing."

"All right."

Happier than he had any right to be when her only interest in him was to teach him something, he smiled. "We'll have dinner—my treat."

By the frown lines between her eyebrows, he knew she didn't like the idea. "Friday night, dinner included—this is sounding more and more like a date."

He wished, devious dog that he was. If he wanted to be around her, it had to be on her terms. "Not a *date* date. You're giving up your free time to tutor me. Dinner is the least I can do. Charlie and I plan to work on our project first thing in the morning, so that we can knock off around five. How about five-thirty?"

"Since it's Petal's turn to close up shop tomorrow night, okay."

"Petal? That's some name."

"Thank her parents. She's only twenty-two, and she's amazing. Tell me where you want to eat and I'll meet you there."

"I like Mama's Cantina."

"Me, too, and I haven't eaten there in ages."

"I'll pick you up." One look at her raised eyebrows and he added, "No sense in us both driving, and I'll be coming from the hangar and already in my car..."

"Why not? You can come to Second Hand Rose and take a look at the lamps. Maybe while I'm waiting, I'll get some of my paperwork done."

"You have a lot of it?"

"Endless amounts, but it's part of the job and the business."

"I hear that. Between firefighting and the plane business... You wouldn't believe the reports, forms, and records we need to keep." He nodded at his Expedition. "That's mine."

"I'm the silver Honda over there. See you tomorrow night."

Nate whistled all the way home.

～

CONSIDERING that Nate and Charlie had removed the guts and insulation from the Learjet's interior, reinstalled fresh insulation and high-end paneling, and prepped a bunch of other stuff for later, the hangar looked surprisingly clean.

Carpeting, shelving, and other building supplies they'd purchased were labeled and laid out neatly along one wall. Bulging trash bags secured with ties sat ready for the garbage bin outside, and the growing pile of materials ready for the dump had been loaded into their old truck, ready for disposal.

Between Nate's training as a firefighter and Charlie's inclination to tidy up as he went, the end of the day cleanup tended to be a breeze.

As they prepared to lock up the building they co-owned, Charlie eyed him with disbelief. "I can't believe my sister's giving you lessons about women."

"What's wrong with that?" Nate hefted two trash bags, Charlie grabbed two more, and they headed for the dumpster outside. "Like I keep saying, I need all the help I can get. Becca and I talked about it after the meeting last night. She agreed to help me out. In return, I'll treat her to dinner at Mama's Cantina."

"Scarlett and I eat there a lot. Sounds like a date to me."

"Becca's not into me that way."

"You sure about that?"

Unfortunately. "As far as I know. Unless she said something to you."

"Nope, but with my sister, you never know. She's real private about her feelings." Charlie's phone signaled a text. He grinned at the screen. "Good thing we're done here. In the summer, the city planning department closes early on Fridays. Scarlett wants me to hurry my butt home right now."

Nate envied the guy. "City planners have all the luck. Why don't you sleep in tomorrow? I'll come in early and head for the dump."

Back-to-back, twenty-four hour shifts Mondays and Tuesdays at the fire department meant that Nate sometimes spent his weekends at the hangar, especially when he and Charlie had to work against a deadline. With the wedding in seven weeks, he couldn't take a day off, even if he wanted to. Charlie also planned to work Saturday and part of Sunday.

"Thanks, man. I could use an extra hour or two of shut-eye, and I know Scarlett will appreciate it." Charlie winked. "Enjoy that lesson tonight."

4

L eaving Petal to deal with customers, Becca sat in her office in the back, supposedly whittling down her pile of paperwork. Mostly, she thought about the upcoming evening. Nate wanted information on resolving a disagreement before it spiraled into an argument. A pro at sidestepping conflict, she was happy to share what worked for her. Not that her skills had done her any good. She was still single. And happy about it, she reminded herself.

But still crushing badly over Nate, even if their approaches to relationships were polar opposites. He was as indifferent to her as ever—except as a resource to help him with women.

Shortly before he was due to pick her up, she rejoined her assistant. At five-thirty on the nose he pulled into the parking lot. Standing out of view, Becca and Petal stared shamelessly as he exited his car and made his way toward the entrance of the shop. He had the long, easy stride of a man secure with who he was, and that made him a pleasure to watch.

Petal murmured in appreciation. "For an old guy, he's hot—even better-looking in person than in the firefighter calendar photo."

She considered anyone older than thirty over the hill.

"Thirty-four isn't old," Becca said. "It's a year younger than I am."

Fiddling with her nose ring, Petal studied her. "You look pretty good for your age."

"Thanks. I think."

The bell over the door tinkled as Nate sauntered inside. "Hey," he greeted, with a mesmerizing grin that set Becca's heart thudding even if she wasn't in the market for a man.

He trained that beacon of warmth on her normally talkative assistant, who suddenly seemed at a loss for words. "You must be Petal. I'm Nate."

"You've heard of me?"

"Becca mentioned you last night. She thinks you're great."

The younger woman beamed. "Thanks, Becca."

Nate glanced around. "This place is nothing like I remember. Looks like a lot of cool stuff."

Becca smiled. "We think so. Petal, will you show Nate the lamps while I grab my purse?"

When Becca returned to the front area of the shop, Petal's eyebrows raised dramatically, likely because she'd put on lipstick and fixed her hair.

"So, are you two, like, going on a date?"

Becca nearly died on the spot. "No. Did you find a lamp, Nate?"

"Not yet." He turned to Petal. "Becca's helping me out and I'm treating her to a dinner."

"I'm so embarrassed," she mumbled as they headed for his Expedition.

"Would going out with me be that bad?"

"Well no, but we aren't exactly..." She struggled for the right word. "Suited to each other."

He didn't reply. Why would he, when he no doubt agreed?

It was a warm evening and the sun was beginning its path toward the horizon.

"How was your day?" he asked as he headed the car toward the road.

"About what I expected—slow but not dead. How about yours?"

"Charlie and I accomplished a lot, but we're in for a long weekend."

"Even Sunday?"

"Until we finish the plane."

Becca nodded. "Because of the wedding."

"Right. Look at this traffic."

"It is rush hour and the height of tourist season."

"And everyone in town is on the road. At least it seems that way."

"Are we in a hurry?"

"If we want to make our six o'clock reservation."

"You reserved a table?"

"I don't want to waste a minute of your valuable time."

Such a considerate man. Becca felt warm all over.

They arrived at Mama's with a few minutes to spare. As the hostess showed them to the table, women all over the restaurant shot envious looks at Becca. In their shoes, she'd have done the same.

Moments after they slid into opposite sides of their booth, a middle-aged waitress appeared. In her eagerness to reach them, she almost tripped over her own feet.

"You're Mr. August," she gushed, even more flustered than Petal had been.

Nate grinned. "That's me. What's your name?"

"Carol."

"Good to meet you, Carol."

"You, too. We have a copy of the calendar on the wall in the back room. Will you sign it?"

"Sure."

"Thank you! I'll bring it to you with your drinks."

Ten minutes later, Nate had autographed the calendar and showered Carol with another lethal grin. She almost floated away.

"You're a natural at making women feel valued and attractive," Becca observed. "You're also good at dealing with adoration."

"Didn't used to be, but since we published

that calendar... A guy gets used to the attention. It's for a worthy cause, right?"

"Absolutely." The firemen's benefit fund had helped countless locals who'd lost homes and possessions to fire.

"Tell me about tonight's lesson," he said.

Between the restaurant's spicy Latin music, chattering diners, and the clatter of cutlery, Becca had to raise her voice. "If you really want to learn how to deflect an argument, we should do some role playing."

"Say what?" Nate cupped his hand with his ear.

She repeated the comment.

"I didn't think about the noise level in here," he said. "We need a quieter place to work. After dinner, we'll find something."

They enjoyed a pleasant meal, first shouting to be heard, then pantomiming, which led to a great deal of laughter. It'd been a long time since Becca had enjoyed herself this much.

By the time Nate signaled for the check, she was relaxed and ready for the lesson.

～

"I MUST BE GETTING OLD," Nate said as he and Becca headed for his Expedition after the meal. "The noise level in Mama's never bothered me until tonight." In the sudden quiet outside, his ears rang.

"Some restaurants want loud noise, so people to come in to eat and leave quickly instead of lingering to talk. Think how many more customers they can serve. We sure laughed a lot, though."

He grinned. "When you bit into that taco and everything squirted out the other end?"

Becca cracked up, and he joined in. He felt so comfortable with her. Also turned on. What guy wouldn't be? She was something special.

He started to slip his arm around her, then stopped himself. She wasn't into him that way.

"It's a good thing I was leaning over my plate," she said. "Otherwise, I'd have a nasty stain on my outfit."

Dusk was fast fading into night, the last rays of the sun streaking red across the sky. Nate took in Becca's summer dress, a sleeveless, pale pink affair that hugged her curves just enough, and shook his head. "That would've been a shame."

"You're telling me. I bought this dress last month, and I've only worn it a few times. Can you imagine me in the bathroom, frantically rubbing cold water all over myself, and finishing the meal drenched?"

He could, and that stirred up all kinds of trouble in his body. He shut that train of thought off. "You mentioned role playing."

"So that you can practice what you learn. We'll pretend we're a couple on the verge of an argument."

"I can do that, no sweat." God knew, he'd had more than enough experience.

"All we need now is a place."

"It's tourist season. There are plenty of coffee shops still open tonight."

"I don't know, Nate. It's probably better if people don't hear you yelling."

He didn't want her getting the wrong idea about him, and pulled her to a halt. "Hold on there. FYI, I'm not a man with a hair-trigger temper. It takes a lot to make me angry."

"Which is a good thing, but just in case, I think we need privacy."

Nate disagreed. With his raging attraction to Becca, being alone together was a bad idea. "Why don't we role play in the Expedition?" he asked as he unlocked the doors.

"Do you see all the people coming and going from this restaurant? What if someone we know sees or hears us? I don't want anyone thinking we're really fighting."

"We'll keep the windows up and the air blasting—like so." He started the engine and cranked up the AC.

"People can see through the windows."

"It's almost dark. If they're nosy enough to peer inside, they'll see two people engaged in conversation."

"I'm not role playing in this car," she said.

"Up to you. Your place or mine?" If they stuck to the lesson, he'd behave himself.

"Neither."

"Second Hand Rose?"

"Friday is the only night we're open until nine, and that's almost a whole hour from now. I wouldn't want Petal hearing us." She frowned. "Why did you buckle up?"

"You should, too. We're outta here."

"But we haven't decided where we're going."

"At least we'll be moving. Better than being stuck here listening to you shoot down all my suggestions."

"I wouldn't if I thought they were any good."

"I don't hear you coming up with alternatives."

Becca opened her mouth, and Nate figured she'd snap at him. Instead, she drew in a deep breath, exhaled, then did it again. After that, she seemed more relaxed.

"You stopped arguing altogether," he said. "Okay, I get it."

"That's just one technique. Let's both try to think."

As they tooled up Kirkdale Road in the deepening night, he wracked his brains. Up ahead, a barely noticed narrow dirt road cut through the trees. That'd work. Signaling, he angled onto it.

Her head swiveled to the windshield. "This looks like a road to nowhere."

"Pretty much. You don't want anyone to see us, and God forbid someone overhears us."

"It's role playing, remember? When I mentioned privacy, I didn't mean out here in the boonies."

"We're here, and it meets all your restrictions. Let's get started."

She gaped at him, as if he'd uttered gibberish. "I can't do it here. I'm not comfortable in the woods at night. Besides, it rained a few days ago, and when that happens mosquitoes show up.

"Plus, I don't see anyplace where we can turn around to get out of here. And what if you run over something sharp, like a rock or a broken bottle or a nail, and blow a tire? It's pitch black outside, and the cell phone reception out here isn't always—"

Enough already. Nate slammed on the breaks, popped off his seatbelt, and cupped her shoulders. "Hush, so I can kiss you."

5

_____

N ate was going to kiss her. Startled into silence, Becca let him. He brushed his mouth over hers. She meant to push him away, but her hands got mixed up, grabbing fistfuls of his shirt, and tugging him closer.

After more than eighteen months without a man's touch, her entire body rejoiced in the sheer pleasure of his attention. And not just any male. *Nate.* She forgot about role playing, forgot that they weren't involved and shouldn't be and locked into one of the best kisses of her life.

Proving he knew a great deal about what he was doing, he cupped her head between his big hands and slanted her chin enough to deepen the pressure of his lips. She didn't want him to ever stop.

All too soon, he broke away. When she craved more. "That was unexpected," she said, marveling that her longtime crush had finally kissed her. Even if he was just being his popular playboy self in the middle of the woods, the whole experience was so worth it.

"I couldn't think of any other way to shut you up. You were on a roll with no end in sight."

She had to laugh. "I was, wasn't I? Your scheme worked." And then some. Her lips still tingled.

Avoiding his scrutiny, she dipped her head to her phone and checked the time. "We both have to get up in the morning, and it's too late for a role play. Do you have any idea how to get out of here?"

"If I didn't, I wouldn't have come this way, let alone parked here. About ten feet ahead, the road loops back around to the highway." He eased the Expedition forward.

"How do you know about this place?" she asked.

"This is where I used to bring girls to make out."

She laughed again. "So you planned to make out with me tonight?"

"No—honest. I didn't even know where we'd end up until I recognized the road."

They made the drive to Becca's shop in comfortable silence. Petal had closed up, and Becca's was the only car in the lot.

"Too bad about the role playing," she said as Nate pulled up beside it.

"That's okay. What we did was a lot more fun."

He was playing with her, and she gave him a teasing shove. "You're such a guy."

"You like me, though."

She wasn't going to admit how much. She was so not his type. "You're okay. You asked for my help and treated me to dinner, but I still owe you a lesson. Next time we'll talk techniques instead of actually role playing. Then I can tutor you anywhere."

"You're offering to do this again?" His grin told her he liked the idea. "Thursday and Friday evenings are best for me."

"I'll check my calendar and get back to you."

"Do that."

In the light from the dashboard, his eyes seemed to glitter with heat. She expected another kiss, but he surprised her with something different, giving her cheek a soft caress with his thumb. "Good night."

He wasn't the first man to do that, yet with him, the gesture felt oddly intimate. Such a small thing to make her heart lift in her chest. Becca waved and slid out of the car.

Nate stayed where he was until she started the engine and flipped on her headlights. Then, with a light tap to his horn, he took off.

∾

NATE SPENT a quiet afternoon at the station Monday, a nice respite after a morning of medical emergencies and a house fire. After dinner, taking advantage of the light breeze, he and Ethan, Rob, and Liam hauled a folding table and four chairs through the open apparatus bay to the lighted area outside. There, they sat down and played Yahtzee. The previous year, Rob had gotten them hooked on the game.

As always, Nate played to win. But today he lost twice in a row.

Ethan, the top scorer, crowed over his win. "When you spring for the doughnuts in the morning, bring me one, no, two chocolate glazed."

Rob and Liam chimed in with their requests.

"Since when did we decide the loser catered to special orders? Expect the usual assortment," Nate said, but his good-natured grin ruined his tough-guy reply.

Ethan eyed him. "You're way too happy about coming in last. You clocked in this morning like that, and after spending all your time off working on that plane."

"Not all my time. I took Friday night off."

"You didn't show at the poker game. What's her name?"

"Becca Chambers."

"Charlie's sister? She's cute. No wonder you're in such a good mood. When did that happen?"

"We met up at the planning meeting for his wedding."

Ethan nodded. "Does he know you're seeing her?"

"It's not what you think. She's a friend. I told her I needed help understanding women, and she agreed to give me pointers. That's why we got together Friday night. And yeah, Charlie knows."

Nate's buddy scrutinized him. "Did she tell you anything useful?"

Nate made a so-so gesture with his hand. "We're moving in that direction. I need a lot of help."

"We all do."

"You?" Nate hooted at Ethan. "Every time you wail on that sax of yours at a concert, women throw themselves at you."

"Doesn't mean I understand them. What've you learned?"

The other three crewmates stilled and trained their gazes on Nate.

That he liked kissing Becca and wanted more. But he wasn't going to talk about that. "For starters, women like to be heard." Becca had offered that valuable nugget the night of the planning meeting.

Rob grimaced. "Don't I know it. No matter what I do, I always fall short." Divorced, with twin teenage daughters, the poor guy didn't stand a chance.

Frowning, Liam ran his hand over his shaved head. "We all have ears. We know how to nod and make appropriate comments. What are we missing?"

Equally clueless, Nate shook his head. "I'll ask her to clarify that at our next lesson."

"You convinced her to give you another one?"

"She realizes how bad off I am. We're mostly going to work on dealing with conflict before it turns nasty."

"You sure this is a friends-only thing?" Ethan asked as they returned the die and score pads to the Yahtzee box.

"All right, I like like her. But it's not reciprocal." Although after that hot kiss he wondered.

"Maybe after you learn a thing or two and smarten up, she'll come around."

Time would tell.

6

Tuesdays, the one day of the week Becca's shop was closed, she ran errands, cleaned house, bought groceries, and took care of other personal chores. Today there was no time for the usual routine. Scarlett's wedding dress was ready for a second fitting, and she wanted Becca's opinion. If that wasn't fun enough, Becca's maid of honor dress had also arrived.

In a flurry of excitement, she drove to Patrice's Bridal Shop to meet her friend. At eleven o'clock, Patrice Regan, the statuesque owner of the shop, ushered them through the door for a private appointment.

While Patrice helped Scarlett into her gown, Becca held up her own dress—strapless—and studied herself in the full-length mirror. A full-busted woman, she preferred the reassurance of straps, but with the right bra she'd no doubt manage.

She'd never considered wearing burnt orange, either, but had to admit the color suited her. After dieting for weeks, she hoped the dress fit. Soon enough, after Scarlett's fitting, she'd know.

"Coming out," the bride-to-be announced as Patrice pulled the dressing room curtain open.

With small, careful steps, Scarlett emerged and moved to the viewing platform. There, the alterations woman helped her into her wedding shoes, and then arranged the skirt of the dress so that the hem fell into place at her feet.

"What do you think?" Scarlett asked, biting her lip.

The dress, a sophisticated affair with tiny pearls and touches of lace on the bodice, seemed made for Scarlett's petite, slender form. Between the gown, her round blue eyes and thick blond hair, she was breathtaking.

Becca was totally jealous—even if she had made peace with being single. And so happy for her friend. She clasped her hands over her heart. "I think Charlie's eyes will pop out of his head."

Scarlett glowed with pleasure. "I think so, too. I can hardly wait."

Studying her with a critical eye, Patrice conferred with the alterations woman. "It needs to come in a bit at the waist, I think."

"I agree," the woman said. "Otherwise, the fit is perfect. Even the length, as long as she wears those shoes."

After they marked the dress, Scarlett changed back into her street clothes, and Becca stepped into her own dressing room. Thanks to the strapless bra Patrice found for her, her breasts felt secure and didn't threaten to spill out of the dress. The waist also fit, even had wiggle room in case she regained the five pounds she'd shed. Which was great news.

"I would never have picked this dress for myself," she told Scarlett. "But, wow! I feel pretty."

"You look fantastic," her friend said.

"Why didn't your mom come with you?" Becca asked as she and her friend made their way toward the payment desk.

"I didn't invite her. She's too anxious about the wedding. I never realized she was such a micromanager. She has an opinion on every single detail, and it's driving me crazy."

In Scarlett's shoes, Becca knew she'd feel the same. Still... "I love your mom! And you are her one and only. You may as well enjoy."

Scarlett blew her bangs out of her eyes. "I'm trying, but at times like this I wish I had a sibling or two to deflect some of the attention. I don't care if the tables at the reception are round or rectangular. I just want to marry Charlie. I can't wait."

"He's just as eager as you. I'm certainly over the moon. Who'd have guessed one of my oldest and closest friends would marry my brother?"

Scarlett laughed. "It only took us seventeen years to get here."

"You didn't start dating until three years ago. The important thing is, you found each other. I'd bet my business your marriage will be every bit as solid as your parents'. They've always been great role models for me. You know how awful my parents were, screaming and fighting about anything and everything. I've always been awed that yours never fought."

Scarlett gaped at her. "Where'd you get that idea?"

"In all the time I spent at your house, I never heard them exchange a harsh word. They had discussions instead, and that made a huge impact on me."

"It's true they rarely fought, but they had their moments." Scarlett made a face.

The conversation stopped while they settled their accounts, then resumed as they left the air-conditioned shop and stepped out into the brutal heat.

"I'm having trouble picturing your parents in a fight," Becca said.

"You wouldn't if you'd been there."

"What did they fight about?"

"Different things." Scarlett paused and looked thoughtful. "Here's one I'll never forget. I was maybe ten. It was a hot summer day like today. We packed a picnic and went to Guff's Lake to swim.

"We played in the water for a long time, cooling off and having fun. When we got out, Mom put on her beach cover-up, grabbed the picnic basket, and slid her feet into her flip-flops. Unfortunately, a bee had landed on the sole of one. It stung the bottom of her foot, and it really must have hurt.

"Dad sat her down and tried to help, but somehow he made it worse. She was in such pain and so upset, she screamed at him in front of everyone. I was so embarrassed.

"We never did have the picnic. Dad and I steered clear of her for a while afterward, but that didn't help at all. For the rest of the day, she refused to speak to him. She froze him out, he tip-toed around her, and they both forgot about me. I remember hiding in my room, miserable and scared to death they'd get a divorce."

How many times had Becca's parents threatened to divorce each other? So often, that she and Charlie had wished they would, if only to get peace and quiet at home.

"Did either of them threaten divorce?"

"No, but I worried anyway. By the next morning, they'd made up and all was well. Still, the whole thing shook me. Talking about it brings back that sick feeling in the pit of my stomach."

"I know it well."

"Your parents are fine now, right?" Scarlett asked.

"More or less." Not long after Becca had

moved out after high school they'd started seeing a marriage counselor. They no longer constantly tore into each other, but they'd never have the warmth Scarlett's parents shared. "They haven't quit fighting altogether, but at least when they get into it I don't have to hear them."

"My parents haven't stopped, either."

Becca frowned. "Where did I get the idea they never fought?"

"It wasn't something I liked to talk about. Charlie and I fight sometimes. Everyone does, right? A good argument can clear the air like nothing else."

Nate had said that too, and Becca gave Scarlett the same reply. "I wouldn't know—I don't do it."

"Then you're one in a million."

"I'll take that as the highest compliment," Becca said, smiling. "Thanks for inviting me to get a sneak preview of you in that dress. You're going to make a beautiful bride."

After they exchanged hugs and parted ways, Becca continued to mull over the surprising bit of information Scarlett had dropped about her parents. Hard to believe, but it changed nothing.

Each to her own, and Becca wanted no part of fighting. She couldn't even think about it without shaking inside.

～

"I GET that women want to be heard," Nate said when he and Becca met at the Coffee Shack for their second lesson. Located near Guff's Lake Resort, the Shack tended to be busy year-round, but not on a beautiful summer evening. "How do I show that I listened?"

Her brows drew together. "I thought we were going to talk about how to stop a fight before it happens."

"That, too."

"But what you're asking about is a whole different lesson."

He got lost watching her mouth.

"What are you staring at?" she asked.

He jerked up his gaze. "You have a great mouth."

"Do I?" Her fingers fluttered to those perfect lips and for a moment, her gaze softened as if she remembered the amazing kiss they'd shared. Then, like a stern tutor, she straightened her shoulders. "Stop a fight or show a woman you heard her—pick one."

"I don't see why we can't cover both." His buds wanted the information and so did he. "Seems to me they're connected."

"So you *were* paying attention. Not that I could tell from your warm expression."

"Can I help it if your mouth turns me on?"

"Men," she muttered. "Not everything is about sex."

"I realize that." She snorted in disbelief, and

he added, "I don't think about it all the time. Not every second, anyway."

"Hard to believe, when you get that heavy-lidded, sexual gleam in your eyes. If you want to show me you're listening, keep your gaze level with mine and respond in a way that proves you heard me. No checking out my body parts."

Nate followed her instructions. Trouble was, her eyes were big and pretty and easy to get lost in. He forced himself to think about something else. Her hair sure was shiny. Was it as soft as it looked? He itched to pull off that tie that held it back, run his fingers through it, and find out... Better think about something else. *Lalalalala.*

She sat back and crossed her arms. "I'm waiting for a response."

Right. "I'm not thinking about sex now."

Not totally.

He must've convinced her. She unfolded her arms and nodded. "Much better."

Coming from her, high praise. He wanted to grin, but this was serious stuff. He remained solemn. "Tell me how to stop a fight."

"Step one, notice when you're getting angry. The first signs of that begin in your body. On a physical level, what happens when you get mad?"

Nate thought about that. "I tense up."

"In what ways?"

"My gut gets tight. My jaw, too."

"Two good examples. Be aware when those

things happen. Then get rid of the tension before it escalates and you start arguing."

"How do I do that?"

"Well, when I feel myself getting tense, I take a deep breath through my nose. Then I slowly exhale out my mouth and release my anger."

Skeptical, he eyed her. "And that really works for you?"

"Not always. Sometimes I need two or three breaths and a silent reminder that getting mad won't help anything."

"I don't know that I agree," Nate said. "I need to let my anger out. It's how I relieve my tension."

Her soft mouth went tight with disapproval. "If you do that, how are you going to stop a fight?"

She had a point. "How did you learn this stuff?" he asked. "Did you take a class?"

"I probably should have. Growing up, I figured it out as a matter of self-preservation."

"I never had to worry about that. My parents have never been lovey-dovey, but they got along all right."

"Lucky you."

"I never thought about it, but I guess so. I know myself, and a few big breaths won't stop me from being pissed off. For that to happen, I need to clear the air. I need suggestions how to do that without losing my cool."

"There is another tool I use." She leaned toward him as if to impart crucial advice.

All ears, he waited.

"I act as if everything is fine until it is."

This made zero sense to Nate. "I'll take your word for it."

He knew he'd always let Becca have the last word. Maybe that was the key—finding someone you didn't feel like arguing with in the first place. Too bad she wasn't remotely interested in him.

7

"Thanks for the lesson," Nate said, opening the Coffee Shack door and following Becca out.

She glanced up at him, her eyes dark in the twilight. "Did it help?"

"Sure did."

God, he wanted to kiss her. Instead, he waved, climbed into the Expedition parked adjacent to the Honda, and waited for her to back out.

The lot was crowded and she was cautious, inching her way out. Suddenly, a white car sped by and clipped her rear fender. Nate winced at the loud scraping noise, and Becca jumped from the Honda, no doubt to talk to the driver and exchange insurance information. But the car at fault raced for the exit.

"Stay put," Nate told her through his open window.

He followed the vehicle and pounded his horn, to no avail. The heedless driver was about to turn onto the highway and escape. Gunning the engine, Nate pulled into the lot's entrance lane. He shot in front of the other car, blocked its path, and braked to a stop.

He didn't breathe again until the white car squealed to a stop a mere hair's breadth from the Expedition. After quickly putting on his flasher lights, Nate exited. Moments later, he motioned for the driver to put his window down. Loud music filled the car, which explained why the guy didn't hear Nate's horn.

A kid who looked about seventeen stared up at him with wide, frightened eyes. "Turn that radio off," Nate ordered. When the noise shut off, he introduced himself. "I'm Nate," he said, using an easy but firm tone. "What's your name?"

"Webster."

"I want you to slowly and carefully back up, Webster, park your car, and get out."

"Okay." The boy complied.

Nate parked beside him. He wasn't as tall as Nate, but someday he likely would be. "Come with me." He led Webster to Becca, who was watching the whole thing, along with several other people.

"This is Becca," Nate said. "Webster here had the radio up loud." He eyed the boy. "Surely you felt something when you clipped Becca's car. Why didn't you stop?"

"It didn't seem like a big deal. And..." Webster

kicked at a loose pebble. "I didn't know what to do."

"You look awful young to be driving by yourself."

Webster stiffened. "I have my learner's permit. I know what I'm doing. My parents went out tonight. I wanted coffee, so I borrowed my mom's car."

No doubt, the woman was going to be seriously pissed. "She needs to know about this," Nate said. "You call her, and I'll contact the police." A kid driving alone without a regular license meant a ticket and at the very least, an extra fine.

"Do we have to? I don't want to get in trouble."

Nate nodded his chin at the family car's front dented and scratched fender. "Too late for that."

"It was a minor accident—I'm fine," Becca assured Nate while they waited for a police officer and Webster was forced to talk to his parents. "You don't have to stay here with me."

"Maybe I want to."

As good as his word, he stuck by her side through the entire event.

Nate had been firm with the teenage boy, without talking down to him. Unlike Webster's parents, who were understandably furious. He'd likely be grounded for a long time.

Becca accepted his tearful apology and ex-changed insurance information with the couple.

By then, the officer arrived and did his thing. Ticket and hefty fine for driving alone with a learner's permit in hand and head bowed, Webster sat in the white car's passenger seat. His father drove away, his mother following in the other car.

Soon, everyone had left except Nate.

"Thanks," she told him. "You were amazing."

To her surprise, the usually self-assured male ducked his head as if embarrassed. "I didn't do much."

"I disagree. If you hadn't reacted with light-ning speed, Webster would've gotten away with his bad driving. Yes, his parents would've noticed the fender, but they wouldn't have known about the damage to my car. What can I do to thank you?"

He didn't even hesitate. "Give me another lesson."

"Seriously?"

"Hey, you're teaching me a ton of useful stuff."

Flattered, she readily agreed. "Okay. How about next Thursday?"

"I'm thinking sooner. Saturday night."

Date night? She angled her head at him. "Why would you want to spend your Saturday night listening to me talk?"

His gaze went straight to her mouth, and her wayward lips tingled in anticipation. Then, all business, he shifted his attention to her eyes, exactly as she'd taught him.

As pleased as she was that he'd paid attention, she was also disappointed. Couldn't he show a little interest in her? She shouldn't want that—and yet, she did. Even temporarily. To fulfill her longtime fantasy.

"I don't have plans for Saturday night," Nate said. "If you do..."

"Nothing pressing." Other than channel surfing.

"Great."

By his wide grin, she'd made his day. Well, she was a pretty good tutor.

"I'm ready for some role playing," he said. "In the interest of the privacy you think we need, maybe I should come your place. Unless the idea makes you uncomfortable."

Not anymore. "My house is fine. Do you want to keep working on conflict resolution?"

"I don't know yet. Can I think about that and let you know Saturday night?"

She nodded. "See you then."

8

Nate and Charlie met at the hangar before daybreak Saturday. They needed to put in the extra time, as Bill Brady, their client, insisted they make costly and time-consuming modifications to the design he'd previously approved.

This put them behind where they needed to be if Charlie intended to finish the job before the wedding, and meant spending longer days at the hangar. But Brady had offered a hefty premium to get what he wanted, so they went along with it.

"What's on your agenda tonight?" Charlie asked as they closed up shop.

"Another lesson from Becca."

"On a Saturday night." Nate's bud snorted.

"I don't have plans and neither does she, so what's the big deal?"

"You usually play pool, or go out for pizza and beer, or something like that. But a lesson?" Charlie eyeballed him. "You're into my sister."

Seeing no reason to lie, Nate nodded. "You okay with that?"

Charlie grinned. "Hell, yes."

"She's hard to read. I can't tell if she's interested in me, so don't say anything to her or Scarlett."

"Are you kidding? I wouldn't touch that with a fifty-foot ladder. Have fun with that lesson."

After stopping for takeout, Nate went home to clean up and figure out what kind of role playing he wanted to try.

Standing in front of the bathroom mirror, shaving and thinking, he imagined an evening with very little talking involved. He started to get worked up and nicked his chin. "Ouch," he muttered.

Figuring tonight out would be easier if he knew whether she was into him. It took the whole drive to Becca's before he came up with a solid idea for the role playing. That'd work.

He'd never been to her house, but he found it without a hitch. She lived in the south part of town, not far from him, on a street of bungalows and tidy yards. Her place, a white clapboard cottage with rust-color trim, sat smack in the middle of the block.

Seconds after he knocked at her door, she answered. Her hair was pulled into a ponytail and she wore a sundress with thin straps that made him wonder if she was wearing a bra.

"Sure is hot tonight," he said. And not just

from the ninety-degree temperature. "Feels like an oven out here."

"It's nice and cool inside. Come in."

He stepped into a small but comfortable-looking living room with a sofa, armchairs, and colorful prints on the wall.

"What happened to your chin?" she asked.

"I cut it shaving."

"I do that to my legs sometimes. I have beer, wine, iced tea, water..."

"Beer sounds good."

"To me, too. Follow me to the kitchen."

"Did you have any trouble finding the house?" she asked as they moved down a short hallway.

He shook his head. "Turns out, I only live about two miles away."

"Is that right. Strange that we haven't run into each other in the neighborhood. But then, we have different interests, and different friends and schedules."

She opened the fridge. He liked looking at her from the back, liked the way her short dress stretched across her hips and behind as she reached for the beers. Even her sandals turned him on, with their straps as narrow as those on her dress.

"How was work today?" he asked as she pivoted toward him.

"Slower than I'd like, but average for the end of July. I don't buy much this time of year, either."

"What did the auto shop say about your bumper?"

"They have to replace the entire back fender and repaint two panels. It'll be in the shop for roughly ten days. Webster's insurance is paying for it, and his parents are making him reimburse me for the cost of my deductible. He'll pay in installments, using part of his paycheck from his summer job."

"Good deal."

"Yes, and my insurance will cover the cost of the rental car. Thanks to your quick thinking, I'm out nothing."

They clinked bottles and returned to the living room, where they chose armchairs that faced each other across the low-slung coffee table.

Every time she moved, the skirt of her dress rode up her thigh. *Nice.*

While he wondered what kind of panties she was wearing, she tugged the hem down. "What do you want to work on tonight?"

"I need pointers on how to tell if a woman is into me."

"That doesn't sound like role playing, or anything you need to learn. "

"Most of the time I do recognize the signs, but not always. I'd like to run a scenario around that."

"A scenario." Wearing a thoughtful expression, she screwed up her mouth. "Umm..."

"I already thought of a setup. We're on a date

and you act like you're having a good time, but I can't get a true read on you."

She crossed her legs, and that skirt inched up her thigh. Then she fiddled with one of her straps, pushing it up her creamy shoulder. Nate saw no signs of any bra.

"What am I doing?" she asked.

Turning him on more than she'd ever realize. He cleared his throat and stared at the space above her head. "You're engaged in the conversation. You laugh when I say something funny, but beyond that, nothing. No meaningful looks, no touching me, nothing flirty."

"Maybe *you*'re not giving *me* signs and I'm unsure of you," Becca countered. "Are you into me?"

"Definitely." For the first time, he let his gaze travel over every delectable inch of her.

She swallowed audibly. "Maybe we should sit next to each other on the sofa—for the purposes of acting out our role play."

Leaving their beers behind, they moved and sat down. Not close enough to touch, but almost.

Becca reached behind her head to tighten her ponytail. "Don't do that," he said. "Your hair is so pretty. Why don't you take it down?"

Grumbling, she pulled off the tie. "Can we get started now? I want you to show me how you usually indicate interest in a woman."

"First, I'd play with your hair," he said, and combed his fingers through it. "Even softer than it looks."

"I use a good conditioner."

"Next, I'd work on relaxing you." He gently kneaded her scalp. "Does this help?" Her eyelids drifted downward, and he growled in satisfaction. "Feels good, huh?"

"I have to admit, it does. Who'd have guessed you were so good with your hands?"

Talk about a lead-in. He was considering where to put them next when she tilted her face upward, within easy kissing distance.

No mistaking her interest anymore. "The signs you're sending are clear now."

"Are they?"

"Uh-huh. Remember what happened when I drove into the woods the night we were supposed to role play that first time?" he said, massaging the crook of her neck.

Her eyes remained closed, and a tiny smile played at her lips. "You wanted me to stop talking and you shut me up with a kiss."

"We were hot together. I want to find out if we still are."

He gave her a few seconds to tell him to knock it off and shove him away.

She didn't. He went for it.

~

NATE'S LIPS on hers were every bit as delicious as last time, maybe even more so. Becca felt his deep, potent kiss clear to her knees.

Unlike before, he didn't pull away, barely came up for air. When he did, she tugged him down again. He kissed her like a starving man, and she reveled in meeting his demands with her own hunger. At long last, she was living out her fantasy. For now. As long as she remembered that, everything would be fine.

At some point, he left her mouth for her neck, turning it into an erogenous zone she'd never realized she had. With a sigh, she inclined her head to the side and enjoyed the moist trail of kisses that led to the crook of her shoulder.

She shivered, and Nate let out a low laugh. "You like that."

Instead of replying, she arched up and thrust her breasts forward. His clever hands cupped and fondled.

"You are wearing a bra," he said. "I didn't see straps and wasn't sure."

"It's strapless. I'm too full-breasted to go without, and—"

He toyed with her nipple. Whatever she was saying faded into a moan. Lots of them.

His mouth claimed hers again. At the same time, he slid both palms down her stomach, then over her outer thighs. *Mmm.*

Becca did some teasing of her own, putting her hands under his shirt and up his long, muscled back. He tugged her earlobe between his teeth, setting off all kinds of fireworks.

She wanted, no, *needed* his attention a whole

lot lower, but the frustrating man had parked his hands at the base of her hips. Taking charge, she opened her legs a little. He wasn't getting the message, so she nipped his bottom lip and guided him to her inner thighs.

His low growl vibrated in all her female parts. Then he... Let her go?

She opened her eyes. "Nate?"

"I was right—what we just did confirmed it."

In her haze of passion, she'd forgotten the conversation. "Confirmed what?"

"That the heat between us wasn't a one-time thing. You like me."

Unlike before, this time she didn't even try to deny that.

"What are we going to do about it?" he asked.

Good question. The problem was, she liked him way too much for the brief romance she envisioned. There was no doubt in her mind that he didn't want anything more than that, not with her. Besides, they saw the world far too differently. He didn't seem to mind chaos and she shunned it. They could never work as a couple.

That didn't stop her from wanting him with every atom in her body.

Make the smart decision for her future well-being, or give in to desire? She told him the truth —not all of it, what she felt comfortable admitting. "I don't know, Nate."

"Fair enough. At least think about the next step."

She nodded, and he exhaled as if he'd been holding his breath. Brushing her hair back from her face, he kissed her softly. Then stood. "I'll be in touch."

After he left, she sat on the sofa, not at all clear what her choice would be.

9

Quashing a kitchen fire in a second-floor apartment, rescuing an elderly woman who slipped and fell in her bathroom and couldn't get up, responding to false alarms, a grueling workout at the station's gym on the third floor—just another Monday at Guff's Lake FD.

In between calls, Nate thought about Becca. Saturday night proved she was into him, a definite mood boost nothing could kill.

But the nasty fire Tuesday cast a pall over everyone, and his spirits veered to dark places.

Two teenage boys, bored on a hot summer morning, played a game of chicken in an open field, seeing who could hold a lit match longer before blowing it out. One of the boys burned his finger and dropped the thing without extinguishing it. The tiny flame hit the drought-stricken meadow grass and quickly ignited into a full-fledged fire.

Scared, the kid with the burned finger ran away, later caught. The other boy attempted to stomp out the blaze, a fruitless effort that led to third-degree burns on his arms and legs. He was now in the burn unit at the hospital.

Owen also sustained burns on his shoulder and biceps. As soon as Nate and the rest of the crew obliterated the fire, they and Captain Comings headed for the hospital, where they met up with Owen's girlfriend, Halley, and other wives and girlfriends.

Nate envied the couples. He thought about calling Becca, but they didn't have that kind of relationship. Yet. Today, he wanted that, wanted her more than ever.

The entire group hung around until the doctor placed Owen on sick leave and cleared him to go home. They returned to the station around dusk. The women followed with food, which they set in the firehouse kitchen while the crew readied the fire trucks and aid car for the next call, and showered. After the meal, they grouped around the muted TV and rehashed the day.

"In my entire fourteen years with GLFD, that was the worst brushfire I've seen," Tony said. "When I think what could've happened..."

Nate scrubbed a weary hand over his face. "Thank God, we were able to contain and kill the damn thing before it jumped into the foothills."

After that, no one said anything, too stunned

and drained from the ten-plus hours spent battling the inferno that had ultimately consumed several acres. What had been a picturesque meadow now looked like a war zone.

The awful stench of char and devastation had spread over the city. The mayor urged people to either stay indoors or wear masks outside.

"Look—we made the news." Tony turned up the sound.

Reliving the disaster as segments filmed by a news crew aired hurt like a raw wound. Hank grabbed the remote and quickly ended the torture. "I don't want to think about this anymore. Come on, Deanna, let's go downstairs."

The other couples followed, until only Nate and the dwindling number of unattached men in the crew—Ethan, Rob, Liam, and Daniel— remained.

In the glum silence, Ethan nodded at Nate. "You never said what happened at the Saturday night lesson with Becca. Did you learn how to show a woman we're listening?"

Happy to lighten the mood, Nate nodded. "Keep your eyes on hers instead of her body, and keep your brain out of the gutter."

As he'd anticipated, the guys shook their heads and chuckled. He described the role playing without getting into the details.

"What kind of role play is that?" Ethan said. "We all know how to tell when a woman is interested."

"Not when she gives off mixed signals like Becca."

"I hate when that happens," Rob muttered. "Well, is she or isn't she?"

"I think so, but you know how—"

The voice of Miranda, the secretary/receptionist at the front desk, cut him off. "Nate, you have a visitor."

Him? Wondering who it could be, Nate headed downstairs to the lobby.

WHILE BECCA WAITED for Nate in the fire station lobby, she wondered at herself. Driving over here was so unlike her. But after watching the evening news, she couldn't stay away. Never mind that they were different as night and day, and all wrong for each other. She needed to see him.

As he entered the lobby, where she stood waiting, weariness slumped his shoulders and darkened his expression. Seeming genuinely surprised to see her, he broke into a grin. "What are you doing here?"

Her entire world brightened. "The fire, your crewmate, Owen... How terrible. I had to see for myself that you're okay."

"I am now."

Sweet words. She pulled him into a big kiss, right in front of the suddenly fascinated, thirty-something woman at the front desk. No telling what she thought. At the moment, Becca didn't care.

Nate engulfed her in a hard hug that made her feel safe. And relieved.

As nice as it was to be engulfed in his strength and warmth, she wrinkled her nose. "You reek of smoke."

"One of the perks of the job. I showered and changed clothes. Unfortunately, the nasty stuff we were exposed to clings to the hair and skin. Miranda, this is Becca Chambers."

The woman smiled. "I know who you are. I bought a chair and ottoman from Second Hand Rose. Great store."

Nate eyed the grocery bag Becca had placed nearby. "What's in there?"

Feeling sheepish, she handed it to him. "It isn't much—something I picked up at the grocery."

He opened the bag and peered at the cookies and gallon of milk, and licked his lips. "How did you know I've been craving sugary food? Let's take it up to the firehouse kitchen upstairs and you can say hi to some of the guys. You know them from Adam and Sam's wedding."

Becca glanced around. "I didn't realize you had an upstairs here. Am I allowed into the kitchen?"

"Sure. You've never been here, huh?"

She shook her head. "I never had a reason until now."

"Welcome to my home away from home."

He opened the same door he'd come through and led her toward the rear stairs. On the way, she greeted crew members and their girlfriends, holding each other and talking.

Comforting each other, knowing someone cared... Becca was glad she'd come.

In the kitchen, other firefighters sprawled on couches and chairs. Big, solid guys, each looking utterly exhausted.

"Say hi to Becca. She brought cookies and milk." Nate held up the bag and brought it to the big eating table.

Everyone perked up and joined them. In no time, with the packages of cookies open and milk in all the glasses, the men dug in. They made her feel welcome, and soon, she was nibbling a cookie of her own and chatting as if she'd known them forever.

"So you're giving Nate lessons about women," Ethan said as the cookies quickly disappeared.

"He told you about that?" Becca cast a wary look Nate's way. "What exactly have you said?"

"That you're a good teacher and I'm learning a lot."

Gratified, she flashed him a smile. "For that, you get an A."

"Suckup," Ethan snorted.

Nate stood. "Why don't I give you a tour," he said, pulling her up.

"Watch that guy, Becca."

"Come back anytime," several men called out.

"Thanks."

He took her to the apparatus bay and showed her the fire engines and aid car. She saw the brass pole the crew used to descend to the area quickly, and the uniform and the equipment Nate used to stay safe.

He put his life on the line for the people of Guff's Lake. Her respect and admiration for him grew, until a strong current of hero worship swept her off her feet.

The need to protect herself receded, which scared her. She had to get away from his pull before she did something that propelled her straight into the path of heartache.

"It's time for me to leave," she announced.

She fled.

10

P uzzled over Becca's hasty departure the evening before, Nate clocked out Wednesday morning. Even after a decent amount of sleep—for once, there were no late-night emergency calls—he was still puzzled. Talk about mixed signals...

After a quick trip home to change clothes, he headed to the hangar. While he and Charlie worked on the plane, Charlie wanted to talk about yesterday's big fire. Nate filled him in, then told him about Becca. "She came to the station last night to see for herself that I was okay."

"That's a good sign."

"Maybe. With her, I never know. One minute she's concerned and affectionate, the next, she can't wait to get away from me. She has me tied up in knots," he admitted.

"I'm not surprised. She's my sister and I've never understood her. What's your game plan?"

"I don't have one." Nate knew only that his

feelings for her had grown stronger. "Does Scarlett ever mess with your head?"

"Not the way Becca's messing with yours. But lately, she's been on my case about my long hours here. She wants me to come home earlier and take weekends off, but with the wedding coming up, this is a bad time to slow down."

Nate nodded. "Hell, with or without a deadline, you work like a maniac. So do I. Our clients expect no less."

"Exactly. You don't jerk around a man like Bill Brady. Not when he's shelling out the big bucks. Our most lucrative job yet."

"Scarlett has to like that. Plus, Brady will tell his friends what a great job we did. Word of mouth is the best advertisement we could want."

"Amen."

For the next several hours, Nate and Charlie focused on custom-fitting the nickel-plated trim along the walls. All the while, in the back of Nate's mind, he mulled over what to do about Becca.

By the time they called it quits hours later, he'd figured out his game plan. He'd stop by her place and tell her what he wanted. The step after that depended on her response.

AFTER A SURPRISINGLY BUSY day at the store, Becca was eager to go home and relax. As soon as she hung the Closed sign in the door, she tidied up the shop, which took awhile, then readied the deposit. By the time she headed for the night deposit drop at the bank, darkness had fallen.

On the drive home, she thought about Nate, just as she had from the minute she'd first heard about yesterday's fire.

Who was she kidding? He'd been on her mind since Lucky Joe's. If only her crush hadn't grown into something more... But wishing her feelings away wouldn't change them.

In the house, she kicked off her shoes, shed her dress, and pulled on an old tank top and a comfy miniskirt too short to wear in public. After a quick sandwich, she foraged through the cabinet, searching for something sweet to finish off the meal. She was still looking when the doorbell rang.

Trouble stood in the threshold, a cocky grin on his handsome face. "You're finally home. I stopped by earlier."

"The store was a mess and I needed to straighten up." Far too happy to see him, she crossed her arms. As if that could protect her. "What are you doing here?"

"It's good to see you, too," he muttered. "Gonna invite me in, or just scowl at me?"

"I'm not scowling." She wasn't exactly smiling or welcoming, either. Too apprehensive of her feelings, of bringing him into her home again. "All right, come in."

She led him to the kitchen and gestured him into a chair at the table. Which seemed safe enough—as long as she stayed on her own side. She sat down and folded her hands. "You don't seem as tired as you were at the station," she said. "You must've skipped the hangar today and relaxed."

"Not with the deadline Charlie and I have. I got some rest last night—plus, working on the Learjet isn't as physically taxing as firefighting."

"Still, two full-time jobs. Don't you ever take a day off?"

"Once we finish this plane I will. Can I have a glass of water?"

"Of course." She fixed two glasses of ice water, then brought them over and returned to her seat. "You haven't said why you're here."

"You left the station so suddenly last night, we didn't have a chance to talk."

Becca frowned. "As I recall, we did a lot of talking. I didn't realize we had anything else to say."

"We do."

No telling what was on his mind. She raised her eyebrows.

Nate cleared his throat. "I'll get right to the point. A day like yesterday makes a man reexamine his priorities. It meant a lot when you stopped by. But you baffle me, Becca. One minute, you kiss and hold onto me like you care. The next, you up and leave as if you can't wait to get away from me... I can't figure out what you want."

In a perfect world, *him*. But perfect didn't exist. "What do you want, Nate?"

"A lot more than lessons."

"You mean sex. I'm still undecided."

"Not just sex, although I think about it all the time." To his credit, his eyes stayed on hers. "I want us to spend time together and get to know each other better."

Did he mean it? Her heart did a happy dance. But her mind went the opposite direction. Differences aside, and they were huge, she wasn't that interesting. Once the excitement of new sex wore off, he wouldn't stick around.

"Say something," he said. "You care about me —that's why you showed up at the station yesterday."

"It's true, I've been thinking about you a lot. But I'm happy with my life as a single woman." More or less. Before she'd reconnected with Nate. "Plus, I live a quiet life and I'm really boring."

"You, boring?" He snorted. "I don't think so. You constantly surprise me, you make me laugh, and I always learn something from you."

While Becca absorbed that, he went on. "I get that you're scared. So am I. I'm doing my damnedest to learn how to create something positive and lasting. That's why I asked for lessons. I've never been great at expressing my feelings, but I'm being straight about this. That has to count for something."

"You do apply what you learn."

He nodded. "While we get to know each other, I want you to continue tutoring me. In return, I pledge to hear you and respect you, be open, and keep learning and growing. If we both work at this, we can build something good."

His hope was infectious. She wanted to buy into his dream, but doubt and her unhappy history caused her to hesitate.

Reaching across the table, he cupped her face between his hands and peered intently at her, as if her answer meant the difference between his life and death. "Say you'll see me."

She caved like a house of cards. "You're a difficult man to resist. All right, but no guarantees."

11

Becca had given Nate the green light to start something together. It wasn't a defi- nite, "Yes, I want a future with you," but considering she'd never looked twice at him until recently, he'd take it. He intended to give his all to her and the relationship. Pushing to his feet, he rounded the table and brought her up beside him.

Not great at expressing his feelings with words, he let his kiss speak for him. It quickly melded into another, then more. Before long, she was plastered against him.

He wanted her so much, he could easily lose control. But this wasn't the time. With effort, he tore his mouth away and rested his forehead against hers. "I could use a lesson about now."

"A lesson?" She blinked at him, as if trying to focus.

Knowing he'd put that dazed look on her face felt good. "Tell me what gives you pleasure."

"I think you've figured that out."

"I know what I like." He traced her nipple with his finger, letting out a low laugh when her eyes drifted shut again and she trembled.

"You and me both."

"What else?"

"For that, we should move to the couch."

Moments later, seated side by side, Nate returned to the question. "What turns you on, Becca?"

"Kiss me all over."

"Woman, you're killing me. As you can see." He smirked at his erection. "It's been like this since that night at Lucky Joe's. Prepare to be turned on."

Returning to her mouth, he coaxed her lips apart and used his tongue to tease her. He planted kisses on her neck and shoulder, then tasted the skin along the scooped neck of her tank top. Soft sounds of desire mingled with her heaving breath.

"You okay?" he asked, raising his head.

"I'm good." She wrinkled her forehead. "Why did you stop?"

"I can't kiss you all over if you're wearing clothes. I need instructions."

"You're crazy, know that? Let's take off our tops."

Eyes on each other, they ditched the shirts at the same time. Her nipples strained at the cups of her bra, begging him to touch and taste. He swallowed hard. "Leave that on?"

"Don't you dare."

With unsteady fingers, he unhooked and removed the bra. Her breasts spilled out, full and aroused, and he took a moment to appreciate her beauty.

"Touch me like you did before," she whispered.

He started with his finger, then switched to his mouth and tongue. She let out a moan he wanted to hear more of.

"This is my favorite lesson so far," he said.

"Quit talking and get back to business."

"Yes, ma'am."

Soon, gasping and shifting restlessly, she guided him downward. "Lower."

Desire took over and he forgot about lessons. As he breached her panties, she sucked in an audible breath and arched her hips. Not long after he touched her most womanly place, she climaxed.

When she lay calm again, he kissed her deeply. Then grinned. "I sure aced this lesson. Although I haven't kissed you all over."

"You did just fine." She reached for his zipper. "My turn."

Although his body demanded release, he didn't want to go there yet. "Another time." He caught hold of her wrist and pressed his lips to the sensitive underside. "Tonight was about you."

He left with a lift in his step and a date to see her the following night.

～

HUMMING, Becca left Petal in charge and went home to bathe and dress for her Friday night date with Nate. Over the past ten days, not counting his shifts at the fire department, they'd spent almost every evening together.

Amazingly, they hadn't had sex. Despite giving her a great deal of pleasure, Nate seemed in no hurry for his own. He didn't pressure her at all. She'd never known a man like him.

He didn't know it yet, but that was going to change tonight. They were going to make love.

As always, he greeted her with an ardent kiss and an intimate smile, his eyes all over her. "I like that dress, but it's awful fancy for Harvey's."

Becca wasn't in the mood for pizza or any heavy food, especially on such a hot summer night. "So you're set on pizza tonight?" she asked.

"Oh, yeah."

Where to eat, where to go, how to spend their time together—more often than not, he made those decisions without a thought about her. It was starting to bother her. Would it kill him to ask what she wanted to eat, or where she wanted to go?

She thought about suggesting something, only they were getting along so great and she shied away from making any waves, even minor ones.

In the car, they caught up on the day.

"Charlie and I are making great headway with the plane. We're starting to see the end in sight."

"Then you'll finish before the wedding for sure?"

"If we keep up the pace and Bill Brady doesn't request any more last-minute changes. Hey, why don't you to come and take a look at it when we're done?"

He'd never invited her to the hangar before. "I'd like that. I'm getting excited about Scarlett's shower next Saturday. We're going to have the best time—a whole day at Wanda's new spa, then a nice dinner, and other fun stuff to put a smile on Scarlett's face. As if she needs anything more to smile about."

Chuckling, Nate pulled into the lot at Harvey's. "These days, she and Charlie are wearing matching grins. According to Gus, Wanda put her all into the spa, and it's something else. Charlie's party will be fun, too, but not as classy as the shower."

"Don't tell me you hired a woman to jump out of a cake," Becca said.

"Nothing like that, although Charlie may be arrested by a female 'police officer.' There's a parking spot. Let's go eat."

As usual, Harvey's was busy, but most of the

customers ordered takeout. Becca and Nate didn't wait long for a table. Menu in hand, Nate took charge again, never thinking to find out what she wanted for dinner. Before she had a chance to decide, he'd ordered and the waitress had moved on.

Breathe.

He squinted her. "You okay?"

No, I'm frustrated. "I want a salad," she said, raising her hand to attract the waitress's attention.

"I thought you liked pizza."

"I do. I just... Never mind." What was the point of making a fuss and causing possible problems between them? Becca dropped her hand. "It's fine."

And it was. As always, the restaurant outdid itself with a terrific pizza.

But Becca's irritation continued—with herself for not speaking up more forcefully, and with Nate for not insisting she order the salad. To the point that she no longer wanted to make love with him.

How could a man so solicitous to her physical desires—and he was better than good at that—yet fail to notice her other needs?

As soon as they stepped through her door and shut it behind them, Nate kissed her and touched her, and asked her what she wanted. Her resentment faded in a haze of desire.

When her breathing grew ragged and her body ached for release, she pulled back. "Come with me," she said, tugging his hand.

"You're taking me to the bedroom."

"That's right. This is your lucky night. I even bought condoms."

"You mean it?" He almost dragged her the rest of the way.

Sometime later she lay beside him, sated and content. No complaints in that department.

He kissed the top of her head. "That was worth waiting for."

Becca agreed, already half in love with him. At times like this, she could imagine her and Nate as a forever couple.

How did he feel about her? Although he held her close and treated her with tenderness, he never said.

"I think you like me." She'd heard the same thing from him several times. Underneath her teasing tone, she hoped he'd share his feelings. Because, face it, thanks to her history with men, she was a tiny bit insecure. Make that hugely insecure.

"Yeah, I like you." He played with her hair.

His answer was better than nothing, but fell short of the reassurance she sought. Careful not to sound too needy, she tried again. "You're only saying that because you finally had your way with me."

He frowned as if she'd asked him to calculate

the number of yards of satin in Scarlett's wedding gown. "That sex blew my mind. I also care about you. A lot."

Much better. Becca wanted to melt. Did, in a haze of warmth and happiness. Snuggling against his side, she fell asleep.

12

"**S**uch an amazing day, and what a fabulous new spa!" Scarlett exclaimed as she and Becca, Alexis, and Marissa floated out of Wanda's Spa. "I love you guys!"

"Love you back," Becca said, trading smiles with the bridesmaids for a job well done. Facials, a therapeutic soak in a hot tub, massages, complimentary champagne—could there be a more perfect wedding shower? "It's not over yet. Who's ready for cocktails and dinner?"

In high spirits, they piled into the Uber they'd hired and headed for Cutie Pie, an adorable upscale café with terrific food and an amazing assortment of fresh-baked pies.

"Just think, three weeks from today, I'll be Charlie's wife!" Scarlett squealed, courtesy of the multiple glasses of champagne she'd enjoyed.

She wasn't the only one feeling no pain. The four of them chattered and laughed with abandon.

Scarlett flashed a big grin at Becca. "Now you and Nate are dating. I'd never have put you two together."

"You would if you'd seen the sparks between them the night we planned this shower." Marissa fanned herself. "We should've taken bets, Alexis."

"I certainly never expected it would happen," Becca said. "I wasn't looking to date Nate or anyone else, but I'm glad we're seeing each other. We have a great time together, and he makes me laugh." And the sex got better and better. She couldn't imagine ever growing tired of Nate's loving.

If only he showed more interest in her in other ways... But she wasn't going to think about his lack of concern for what she wanted outside the bedroom or his failure to share his feelings. "He's a good man," she added.

Scarlett gave her a knowing look. "All I know is, you two are spending a lot of time together. Are you getting serious? That'd be so cool!"

"We've only been seeing each other for a month," Becca reminded her. From dateless on purpose to spending most of her evenings with Nate... My, how she'd changed. "I like him, but I'm nowhere near ready to make a commitment."

As true as that was, the idea of a relationship with Nate no longer scared her to death. They had their issues—at least she did—but for the sake of peace and harmony, she preferred to ignore them.

Even if she did spend a fair amount of time frustrated.

"In your shoes, I'd want to be serious," Alexis said. "He seems like such a great guy—plus he's hot." She fanned herself and Becca laughed along with her friends.

"He's a lot more than that," Becca said. "He's a great firefighter who also designs the interiors of private planes. And as soon as he and Charlie finish the upgrades on their current project, I get a tour. I'm excited."

Scarlett's smile vanished. "I'm so sick of that plane. Bill Brady, the multimillionaire who hired Charlie and Nate, is always changing his mind and wanting something different. Charlie goes along with whatever the man wants. I get that Mr. Brady is a customer and Charlie and Nate want him to be happy, but you'd think with the wedding coming up the guy would cut them some slack. At this rate, they'll be working on it forever."

She sounded like a whiny, petulant child—not at all like her usual self.

"Don't forget, he's paying for all those changes," Becca reminded her. "Anyway, according to Nate, they expect to get it done by the end of next week. Then you and I get the grand tour and dinner out. Our first double date. After that, Charlie will be able to concentrate on your wedding."

"I'll believe that when I see it." Scarlett crossed

her arms. "Lately, all I hear is Bill Brady this, Bill Brady that. Charlie spends more time at the hangar than he ever spends with me. I'm beginning to think he loves working on that stupid plane more than he loves me, and you can tell him I said so!"

With her red cheeks and compressed lips, she looked steaming mad. Becca exchanged alarmed looks with Marissa and Alexis, and then attempted to restore her friend's good humor. "Charlie's my brother and you're my best friend, which is why I'm not going anywhere near that," she said in a teasing tone. Then, more seriously, "You're stressed out, Scarlett. Between all the last-minute wedding details and your demanding city planner job, I don't blame you for feeling overwhelmed."

"Oh, it's a lot more than that. But you've put a lot of effort into this shower and I don't want to waste any more time thinking about Charlie ignoring me. Wait till you see the adorable wedding favors I ordered!"

Scarlett pulled out her cell phone and called up the photos. While she passed the phone around, she launched into the story of where she'd found the goodies. Once again, she became the bubbling bride-to-be. Crisis averted and relief all around.

The Uber driver glanced at them in the rearview mirror. "You're certainly getting an earful," Becca said.

"Mostly I'm remembering when my wife and I got married."

"Was it here in Guff's Lake?" Scarlett asked.

He nodded. "Happiest day of my life."

"How long have you been married?"

"Three years. We have a two-year-old son and another on the way. And we've arrived."

After pulling up at the front door of Cutie Pie, he opened the door and let them out. "You ladies have fun tonight." He smiled at Scarlett. "Especially you. Congratulations. I hope you and your husband will be as happy as my wife and me."

She beamed. "Thank you."

ON WEDNESDAY, Becca heard from Nate. He and Charlie planned to apply the final touches to the plane the following day. After a rough two days at the fire department, followed by a full day at the hangar, he was headed home to crash until morning.

"Why don't you drop by the hangar late tomorrow afternoon," he suggested. "I'll give you the tour, and then we'll go out to dinner."

"With Charlie and Scarlett?" Becca hadn't talked to her friend since the shower.

"That's the plan."

Thursday, she left Second Hand Rose in Petal's capable hands and drove to the hangar on the outskirts of town. She parked next to Nate's

Expedition, the only other vehicle in the lot. No sign of Charlie's or Scarlett's cars. Odd.

Nate must have been watching for her. Before she ever knocked, he opened the door and pulled her inside for a kiss that left her breathless.

"I didn't see Charlie or Scarlett's cars outside," she said when he released her.

"Scarlett stopped by earlier, but didn't stay long. Charlie left, too."

"I hope they'll be back in time to go to dinner."

"Scarlett said she couldn't make it."

"I'm disappointed. What happened, do you know?"

"No idea. She didn't have much to say to me or Charlie. She was in a bad mood—tense and not at all interested in the plane. If you ask me, she's spoiling for a fight."

Becca winced. "Let's hope not, although you may be right. Overall, the wedding shower was great, but she did complain that Charlie spent too much time working. She wanted me to tell him so. Can you imagine getting in the middle of that?" Becca shuddered at the thought. "I said no way."

"You're smart to stay out of their business. I'll bet that by now they've probably patched up their differences. We'll double date another time." Nate gestured at the work space. "Come on, I'll show you around."

The brightly lit hangar consisted of one huge

room with a bathroom in the corner. Aside from one wall of neatly ordered shelves and another of photos, there were several white boards filled with notations and diagrams, and blueprints pinned to a large cork board.

"This place is a lot bigger and much tidier than I pictured," Becca marveled.

"We run it like any other first-rate shop— clean and orderly, which cuts down on waste and accidents."

The plane in the middle of the space drew Becca's attention. "Is that what you've been working on?" She read the lettering on the side. "The *Lady Bill*?"

Nate nodded. "The one and only."

"What an interesting name. Is it named for Mrs. Brady?"

"You'd have to talk to the owner about that."

"I can't wait to see the inside."

Nate grinned. "Put these on and we'll go in."

He handed her a pair of disposable booties, donned a pair of his own, and then led her up the steps, into the most gorgeous plane she'd ever seen.

"Wow," she said, taking in the roomy seats and the fancy tables between them. "This is luxurious."

Nate's chest seemed to swell with pride. Who could blame him? He and Charlie had created a thing of beauty.

"I like that some of the seats face each other," she said.

"That's called a club arrangement, and works well for meetings or board games. The sofa along the side seats three, and there's a single chair across from the cockpit. In all, the plane accommodates two pilots and eight passengers."

Becca nodded. "I'm guessing those seats are real leather."

"The best money can buy. Feel free to test one out."

She sank into a chair and sighed. "Comfortable and soft as butter. This is class in spades."

"That's what we aim for. Our clients tend to be fussy, and for what they pay, they should be. The photos on the far wall of the hangar are before and after shots of the *Lady Bill* and other planes we've worked on. Come on, I'll show them to you."

Back in the work area and standing in front of the wall, Becca counted more than a dozen projects. "The 'after' pictures are totally different from the 'before.'"

"I'd hope so."

Becca's admiration and respect grew for what Nate and Charlie accomplished. "I'm super impressed."

Nate made a sound of pure male pleasure, and from behind, folded her in a hug. "I like when that happens."

Delicious heat filled her. Angling her head, she silently invited him to nuzzle her neck.

He indulged, and she sank against him. "You're turning me on."

"Yeah? I'd planned on us getting something to eat and then heading to my place, but that can wait." He pivoted her to face him. "I've never fooled around with a woman in here."

"Is that true?"

"You're the first and only."

She wrapped her arms around his neck. "You sure know how to flatter a girl."

He backed her someplace. She didn't care where, as long as he made love to her.

13

E ager to satisfy the beautiful woman in his arms, Nate kicked a scarred wooden chair out of the way and lifted her onto the table where he and Charlie did their sketching and planning. Not the most comfortable place, but it'd do.

With a wicked grin, Becca crooked her finger at him. "Come here, you."

"You're bossy today," he teased, stepping between her thighs.

She kissed him with the passion he'd come to crave and anticipate. Greedy to bury himself inside her, he shoved her skirt up and stroked his finger across the crotch of her panties.

Her low moan filled the air. "Hurry, Nate."

She was lifting her hip to help him strip off the lacy things when his cell phone chimed. Paying it no mind, he tugged on the elastic.

Becca batted him away. "Don't you think you should answer that?"

"I'm busy. Whoever it is, they'll leave a message. Anyway, the ringing stopped."

"Now it's started again. It must be important."

Grumbling, Nate slid his cell from his pocket. "It's Charlie. Wonder what he wants?" He picked up. "Hey. I'm kinda busy here. Can I call you back?"

His buddy plowed right past that. "I'm losing it, man. Scarlett's spitting mad at me, and I don't know what to do."

Until now, Nate had never heard panic or indecision in Charlie's voice. He made a face at Becca, then shook his head, and she scooted off the table. "Did Scarlett say why she's upset?"

"She didn't have to," Charlie said. "I already know. I'm not spending enough time with her."

"And you're sure that's the reason?"

"Pretty much."

"Did you ask her?"

"I tried, but she's so pissed off, she tuned me out."

This was not good news. "What did you do, Charlie?"

"Nothing different than usual. I swear."

"Well, you must've done something. You need to find out."

"Like I said, she stopped speaking to me."

Nate thought back to his lessons with Becca. "Get her to cool off."

"If I knew how to do that, I wouldn't be talking to you."

"Tell her what she wants to hear."

"Such as?"

Talk about the blind leading the blind. "Anything, as long as she feels better when you say it."

Charlie groaned. "That's all you can come up with?"

He sounded weary and defeated. Nate scratched the back of his neck and searched his mind for a way to help. "Hell, make something up. Doesn't matter what it is, as long as she believes you listened. Remember, your goal is to get her to calm down so you can fix this."

Becca wore a shocked expression, but Nate was too busy spoon feeding Charlie to wonder at that.

He spun away, strode out of her hearing range, and continued the conversation.

BECCA COULDN'T GET over what she'd heard. Had Nate told her brother to *lie* to Scarlett in order to calm her down? He had. Maybe he didn't use that exact word, but his meaning was clear: Say anything to get what you want.

As his long legs carried him to the far end of the hangar, she frowned. Why in the world would he give such bad advice?

Because he didn't consider it bad.

He'd probably used the same tactic on Becca. She thought back over their relationship. Her initial reluctance to get involved, his appeal to her for lessons. Kisses and warm looks she couldn't resist, and then a promise to be open, to hear and respect her, and the dream-come-true claim that he wanted a future with her.

There'd been no reason to doubt him. After all, he was a good man and he seemed sincere.

But he hadn't uttered another word about their relationship or been open about his feelings for her since... since they'd become intimate.

He'd told her what she needed to hear, and she'd given him what he wanted. Then he'd forgotten about any promise.

Suddenly cold, she hugged herself.

Nate and her brother stayed on the phone for a while. Becca could no longer hear his side of the conversation, but she imagined it. *Make her think that what she wants matters. Parrot her words back to her to convince her you listened. Repeat ad nauseam until you persuade her.*

As the minutes ticked by, her anger grew until she shook with fury. At Nate for his despicable behavior and at herself for her gullibility.

What a fool she'd been. She wanted to scream. That she even considered lashing out surprised her. She was a balanced and peace-loving person. Besides, maintaining her cool was all she had left of her dignity.

She had to get out of here now. Grabbing her purse, she swung for the exit. Nate had ended his call and started toward her. Caught, she froze.

"Sorry about that. Charlie's a real mess, and—"

"I'm leaving."

"What for?"

"I have things to do at the shop." Proud of her level tone and self-control, tenuous as it was, she turned toward the door.

"What about dinner and spending the evening together?"

"I'm not in the mood anymore."

As she marched forward, he grasped her arm. "Slow down."

Her hold on her temper slipped. "Take your hands off me."

With a guarded look, he raised his palms and backed up. "What's wrong, Becca?"

She wasn't calm enough to answer that or meet his probing gaze without exploding.

He didn't attempt to touch her again—smart man. Instead, he stepped in front of her, forcing her to stop moving or bump into him.

"Before Charlie called you were all over me. Now you're shooting daggers at me with your eyes and running away. Don't shut me out."

Running away? Clinging to her self-restraint, she replied through gritted teeth. "I'm not running anywhere." Except from the storm brewing inside her. "Excuse me."

She detoured around him—or tried. The stubborn man remained solidly in her path.

"Talk to me," he said.

"Please move, Nate."

"Not until I know what brought this on."

"I'm trying to avoid a fight!" Her voice was so loud, even her own ears hurt.

He winced, but aside from the questioning lift of his eyebrows, didn't budge.

Until she explained, he wasn't going to let her go. She tucked her shaking hands under her crossed arms. In all, she inhaled and exhaled five times before she felt calm enough to speak in a civil tone. "I heard what you told Charlie."

"Okay." It was obvious he had no idea why his words infuriated her.

Becca glared at him. "It's not okay at all. Scarlett isn't some pet that can be calmed down with something Charlie makes up. It's not okay for him to lie and manipulate her to get his way. Or for you."

"You lost me."

Of course, she had. Lying and manipulation were no big deal to him.

Her hold on the last shreds of her temper snapped, angry words flooding out of her like water through a burst dam. "You may not think twice about saying things you don't mean, but it matters to me. I thought you wanted to understand me because you genuinely cared, but what you really wanted was for me to go out with you. You wanted to sleep with me."

He opened his mouth, but she wasn't finished. "You got what you wanted. I hope you're happy, because we're finished."

"That's not true, Becca, and it's not fair. You didn't hear Charlie's side of the conversation. He said—"

"You told him to lie, Nate. That's all I need to know."

Her knees shook so badly, she wasn't sure she could make it to the door without stumbling. Somehow she did.

14

What had just happened? Dumbstruck, Nate gaped at the door Becca had slammed as she'd left. Then he yanked the door open and started after her. Just then, Charlie peeled into the lot, jerked to a stop, and jumped out of his car.

"Didn't expect to see you here," he told Becca. "I need to talk to Nate. Alone."

"You can have him!" She stalked toward her car.

"What's wrong with her?" Charlie asked.

Too torn up to talk about it, Nate shook his head. Charlie had his own problems, and Nate wanted to be there for him. First, he needed to reach Becca before she left, but she was already in the Honda. "Go inside and sit tight," he said. "I'll be back."

He sprinted toward her.

By the time Becca slid into the driver's seat, tears blurred her vision. *Not here, where anyone can see.* She wiped her eyes, then shoved the key into the ignition. Suddenly, her phone rang.

Scarlett. In no mood to talk to anyone, she hesitated. But it was obvious her friend was in trouble. Why else would Charlie have called Nate, then returned to the hangar to talk to him?

For Scarlett's sake, Becca pushed her turbulent emotions deep inside and answered. "What's happened? Charlie—"

"I don't even want to hear his name right now. I'm not sure I want to marry him, either." She let out a sob.

Fighting a sob of her own—why did love have to hurt so much?—Becca swallowed. "Where are you?"

"Standing at your front door. I need you."

That she'd gone to Becca's house, when she knew Becca would be at the hangar, showed how distraught she was. "Don't go anywhere. I'm on my way."

Becca started the car, but Nate was rushing toward her. With a sigh, she stopped and lowered the window. He looked grim, as if he felt as bad as she did. For some reason, that helped.

Barely winded, he leaned in. "Talk to me— please?"

The pleading note in his voice tugged at her aching heart. There went the tears again. With a great deal of effort, she blinked them back. "I can't, Nate. Scarlett just called. She's having second thoughts about marrying Charlie."

Under his breath, he swore. "I'm pretty sure he's going through the same thing."

"We can't let them call off the wedding. They belong together."

"Yes. We have to talk sense into them. I'll stay here with Charlie."

"I'll go to Scarlett."

Nate nodded. "What about us? You don't get to walk away just because I said something that pissed you off."

Don't lose your temper. Pretend everything's fine until it is. Becca had relied on both since childhood, and they'd served her like trusted friends. This afternoon, they'd failed her. She'd blown up at Nate.

Ashamed of her outburst, even if he was at fault, and with her emotions dangerously close to the surface and her best friend and her brother in crisis, she was in no condition to discuss it. "We don't have time for that now," she said.

"All right." He scrubbed his hand over his face, then straightened. "Later, then."

15

W hen Becca turned into her driveway, Scarlett was sitting on the front stoop, picking at something on her shorts. At the sight of her, Scarlett's face crumbled and she stumbled to her feet.

"Oh, sweetie." Becca grabbed her blubbering friend in a comforting hug and held her for a while before they released each other. "Let's go inside."

In the living room, Scarlett plunked onto the sofa and tilted her head back to rest against the wall. She closed her eyes, and was so still she could have been asleep—if not for the occasional hiccups, the result of a hard cry.

"Why are you having doubts about Charlie?" Becca asked, her heart in her throat.

"He doesn't want to marry me."

She'd expected something along the lines of what Scarlett had complained about during the bridal shower—not this. She barely hid her shock. "He so wants to marry you. He loves you."

"I'm beginning to wonder." Scarlett sniffled. "It's okay—as I said over the phone, I don't think I want to marry him, either."

"That's not true and you know it. You dreamed about being his wife long before he proposed."

"I changed my mind."

"Since when?"

"What does it matter? I did."

What could Becca say to that? "Are you sure? If it were me, I'd think about the future. I'd ask myself, do I want to live the rest of my life with Charlie or without him?"

"I don't want to think about that now or talk about this anymore." Scarlett blew her nose. "We haven't touched base in over a week. How are you, and more important, how's Nate?"

She *would* bring him into the conversation. Becca sighed. "Don't ask."

"You're not getting along either?"

"Promise you won't judge me—I yelled at him."

"You, the woman who prides herself on keeping her cool no matter what? He must've done something awful."

It didn't seem wise to share about his advice to Charlie, and Becca steered clear. "There've been small things that bothered me, but nothing like this time. I tried to hold back, but he made me so mad, I couldn't."

"Wow. I wish I'd seen that."

"I'm glad you didn't." Becca stopped short of telling Scarlett she'd broken off with Nate. No sense giving her friend any ideas. A moment later, she added, "You know what? Letting my anger out felt kind of good."

"Didn't I say so?" Scarlett gave her a watery smile. "This is huge for you!"

"In a scary, embarrassing way. I hate that Nate saw me lose control."

"Is that what's bothering you? I doubt you're the first female to yell at him. As I said that day at the bridal shop, from time to time everyone needs to let off steam. Even you. When I'm mad at Charlie, I make sure he knows right away. I can get pretty loud, and at times he does too. Did Nate yell back?"

"I didn't give him the chance to do that or explain himself." Becca half-wished she had, if only to hear his reasons for suggesting Charlie lie. As if anything justified that. Well, maybe something fun, like a surprise party or a special birthday gift.

"That's too bad. Most of the time, venting your frustrations makes you feel better, like letting the pressure out of a tire with too much air." Scarlett bit her lip. "Other times, you feel terrible."

Becca had experienced both emotions at the

same time. Now she felt raw. But she wasn't here to talk about that. She was supposed to help Scarlett realize that not marrying Charlie would be a mistake. "You're good for Charlie," she said. "You keep him in line."

Scarlett snorted. "You mean I drive him crazy with my nagging."

"Not true. When he veers off-course you steer him in the right direction again. Without you, he'd be lost. And he knows it."

"Does he?"

If he didn't, Becca would smack him upside the head. "Absolutely. You'd be just as lost without him."

Scarlett gave a listless shrug. "All I know is, I need space and a quiet place to think."

"Then take it. The wedding isn't for another two weeks—plenty of time for you to sort yourself out." And hopefully come to her senses.

"That's not a bad idea." Scarlett tapped her finger to her lip, and then nodded. "Instead of leaving early tomorrow I'll take the whole day off. Work is really slow, so that shouldn't be a problem. I'll drive up to our family cabin in the mountains and spend the next three days there. My parents aren't using it this weekend. How could they, when my mother is totally consumed with the wedding and the reception?"

"Sounds like the perfect place to go," Becca said. "If you want to talk while you're gone..."

"I appreciate that, but I need solitude." Scarlett checked her watch. "If I want to get there be-fore dark, I'd better run home and pack, pick up groceries at the store, and go. Do me a favor—don't tell my parents where I am. I'll text that I needed to get away. And not a word to Charlie, okay?"

"My lips are sealed."

They both stood, and Scarlett hugged Becca. "Thank you. I'm so lucky you're my best friend."

"I feel the same about you. I love you dearly. Drive safe."

WHEN NATE RETURNED to the hangar he found Charlie pacing the perimeter. "Come sit down," he called out.

His bud didn't so much as pause. All right, then. Nate strode to where he was, fell into step beside him, and waited to be acknowledged.

After a while, Charlie broke the silence. "I'm freaking out here."

"I see that. So Scarlett's still mad at you."

"What else is new."

"Most of the time you get along great," Nate reminded him.

"Not lately. She's on my ass all the time. If she keeps this up?" Charlie plowed both hands through his hair. "I can't handle that."

"You've been together three years—you know she won't. She's always been fairly easy-going."

"Not anymore. I've been wracking my brain, trying to figure out what else I might have done to make her so mad. All I can come up with is the extra time I put in on the Lady Bill."

"Then good news—as of today, our work on that plane is complete. That ought to make her happy."

"Did she seem happy to you when she stopped by earlier?"

Nope.

Charlie picked up the pace. "How does she think we got the job done so fast?"

"We hardly ever put in such long hours. These were special circumstances—an unusually demanding client and the need to finish the job before the wedding. Surely Scarlett understands that."

"You'd think." At last, Charlie stopped pacing. "Becca seemed real ticked off when she left."

"Yeah. She broke up with me."

"Bummer. Be thankful you weren't engaged."

Not much of a consolation for the empty feeling inside.

"It's weird, though," Charlie went on. "Becca never loses control. I wonder what set her off."

She'd accused Nate of being a manipulator and a liar. That hurt worst of all. "Don't ask. By the way, I gave you bum advice before. No matter what, be straight with your woman. In the long run, you'll be happier for it."

"I'm always honest. Becca must trust you a lot."

Nate squinted at him. "Did you not hear what I said? She broke up with me."

"Like I told you before, she keeps her feelings bottled up. Always has. Blame our parents. The way they treated each other messed her up bad. Getting mad and having a fight, especially with a guy she's dating, scares her—maybe enough to break up with you."

Something to think about later. "If you say so. Back to you and Scarlett."

Charlie groaned. "What was I thinking, proposing to her?"

"Don't be a bonehead. You love her, and you want to be with her forever."

"I thought I did, but this whole marriage thing feels like a big mistake now."

While Nate struggled for the right words to say, Charlie added, "I doubt she wants to marry me, either."

Nate recalled Becca's lesson about breathing. "You're all worked up. Take a couple of deep breaths though your nose. Blow them out through your mouth."

"What for?"

"Just do it, Charlie."

His bud inhaled and exhaled several times. "Feel any better?" he asked.

Charlie shook his head.

Crap. "A lot of people get the jitters before

they get married," Nate said. "That's your problem."

"Nope—I think I'm finally coming to my senses. I'm outta here."

"Where are you going?"

"Don't know yet."

"Do you want company?"

Charlie shook his head.

"Okay, but promise you won't do anything crazy. Don't drink and drive, and no hasty decisions."

"What the hell, Nate. You sound like my dad —not that he's ever given me any worthwhile advice."

"All I'm saying is, don't do something you might regret."

"You don't think I should tell Scarlett I want out?"

Nate cringed at the thought. "I wouldn't. Wait awhile and do some serious soul-searching."

But Charlie had pivoted and was headed for the door, and Nate wasn't sure he heard him.

16

While Charlie made himself scarce Nate suffered through his own private hell. He still remembered the moment he'd first laid eyes on Becca. Young and ignorant about things as he'd been back then, he'd somehow understood that his life had taken a momentous turn, that he'd found the woman of his dreams. When she'd shown zero interest in him, he'd pushed his feelings aside.

Connecting with her all these years later, knowing she wanted him as much as he wanted her, had changed everything. He'd started to believe they had a solid chance at a future together.

Instead, she'd broken up with him, basing her hasty decision on his end of a conversation with Charlie. She hadn't heard her brother's desperation or despair, hadn't given Nate a chance to explain.

She'd sure as hell judged him, though. Convicted and dumped without a trial hurt.

Becca never got mad, or so she claimed. Today she had, her eyes flashing and her cheeks stained red from her temper. She'd even slammed the door. According to Charlie, she'd let her feelings out because she trusted Nate enough to show them. Then she'd ended the relationship because both her trust and her outburst scared her.

Did that even make sense?

Mystified and in no mood for company, he jumped on his bike Friday and rode along his favorite rugged trail through the Siskiyou foothills until his muscles ached and he was drenched in sweat. Saturday, he caught up on chores at home, mowing the lawn, scrubbing the barbecue grill and making it gleam like new, re-painting the trim on the house, washing the car. Anything to keep busy.

Charlie didn't call or text. Nate hoped to hell his friend had taken his advice, and that after careful consideration he'd come to his senses and decided to get married, after all.

Had Becca made any headway with Scarlett? Nate had no idea.

Saturday night he couldn't sleep. Becca cared —that much he knew. He felt the same about her. Hell, he loved her. Every minute they spent to-gether, every time they made love, he showed her how much. Surely she knew that.

Yeah, but you never said the words, idiot.

She didn't know. He bolted straight up in bed.

He needed to tell her and try to make things right. Which could backfire big time. She could kick him to the curb all over again.

But damned if he'd let her walk out of his life without a fight.

Forget sleeping. Anxious to plead his case, he rose, shaved, and showered. He was ready at the cusp of dawn, which was way too early to show up at her door. Seated at the kitchen table, he drank coffee and skimmed the Sunday paper, a big waste of time given his inability to focus.

As the first rays of the sun flooded through the kitchen windows, he poured himself a bowl of cereal. He was stirring the dregs with his spoon when Charlie phoned. "Got in touch with Scarlett yesterday," he said, by way of hello. "She was at her family's cabin."

"And?"

"I asked if I could drive up. She said yes. We worked things out last night."

Hearing the satisfaction in his buddy's voice, Nate smiled for the first time in days. "That's great. Are you with her now?"

"I will be shortly—she's warming up the shower—but I figured I'd touch base with you first. What are you going to do about Becca?"

"Tell her I want her back." Nate checked his watch. She'd be up soon. He had just enough time for a quick stop. "Gotta run."

"Good luck, man."

Minutes later, he slid into the Expedition.

~

TIRED AND OUT OF SORTS, Becca lay in bed Sunday morning, wishing she'd scheduled herself to work today. She needed the distraction to keep her mind off Nate.

Maybe she'd surprise Petal, go in later, and give her assistant the rest of the day off. As she slipped into her robe, Scarlett called.

Finally. Crossing her fingers that all was well, Becca picked up. "Are you still at the cabin?" she asked, and then caught her breath.

"That can wait. Why didn't you tell me you broke up with Nate?"

"Because I didn't want— Wait. Who told you?"

"Charlie did, when he came up."

"I swear, I didn't tell him where you were." Becca sat down on the bed. "I haven't even talked to him."

"I told him when he called yesterday. He drove up right away."

"Where is he now?" Becca asked, crossing her fingers that all was well.

"In the kitchen, making breakfast for us."

"OMG, you two made up!" Becca let out a gleeful whoop.

Scarlett laughed. "Isn't it wonderful?"

"Best news ever." Big relief, too. "How did you work things out?"

"I asked myself your question—did I want to

live the rest of my life without Charlie? No way. I want to have his babies and grow old with him. He wants that, too."

As pleased as Becca was for her best friend and her brother, her heart ached. She wanted what they had. With Nate. *Don't go there.* "Do you two know how lucky you are?"

"Yes. Why didn't you tell me about Nate?"

"You had enough on your plate."

"Have you talked to him?"

"No." Becca couldn't contain her heavy sigh.

"You miss him," Scarlett said. "You liked him a lot. I don't understand why you broke up with him."

"I told you how mad I was." Also emotional, irrational, and terrified of her deepening love for him. Becca almost wished she could undo the breakup, but her pride wouldn't let her. Besides —deal breaker—he thought lying to get what he wanted was okay.

"I wish we'd talked about it first," she added, surprised by her own words. "To give him a chance to explain."

"Hold on—I'm walking into the kitchen and putting you on speaker."

With Becca listening, Scarlett filled Charlie in on the conversation.

"Hey, Becca," her brother said.

"I'm awful glad you and Scarlett made up."

"Same here. Gonna tell Nate you changed your mind and don't want to break up?"

Becca hesitated. Could she? If Scarlett's parents fought occasionally and still enjoyed a loving relationship, why couldn't she and Nate?

"Do you want him or not?" Scarlett said.

"More than I can say."

"Then go get him," her friend and her brother chimed in unison.

17

I n a hurry to see Nate, Becca showered and dressed. Wishing she had time to brew fresh coffee, she poured herself a to-go mug left over from the day before. While it heated in the microwave, she made herself a slice of toast, which she held onto between her teeth as she picked up her purse and got ready to leave. She'd eat on her way to his house.

Coffee and purse in hand, she fumbled with the door. "Dammit," she muttered, struggling to juggle what she was carrying and open the thing. But the door inched open before she could.

"Need a hand?" Nate asked, doing it for her.

Her heart lifted. "Thanks. This is a surprise."

"Brought you a coffee—but it looks like you don't need it."

"Oh, but I do. This is yesterday's." She put the toast and day-old coffee on the table in the entry, set her things down, and took the freshly made cup. "Believe it or not, I was about to leave for your house. Come in. It's good to see you. Did you hear about Charlie and Scarlett?"

As Nate stepped into the house, he broke into a grin. "Charlie called earlier. Thank God they came to their senses. So you're glad I'm here?"

There went her nerves. She nodded. "I want to talk to you."

A guarded expression replaced his smile. "Same. You first."

Stalling for time—it wasn't every day she apologized and asked the man she loved to explain himself—heck, she'd never done it—she gestured toward the kitchen. "Why don't we talk in there."

They sat down.

Nate's somber expression made her even more jittery. Cupping the coffee between her suddenly cold hands, she started. "I want to apologize for not giving you the chance to explain yourself. I'm ready to listen."

He exhaled loudly. "Charlie was losing it and I had to talk him down. I said the wrong thing—I knew that before you called me on it. When he came back to the hangar that day, I told him I'd given him bum advice and to always be straight with his woman. I don't lie and I'm not a manipulative man, Becca. I meant everything I ever said to you. You have to believe me."

Hugely relieved but too keyed up to smile, she looked him in the eyes. "I do."

Now for apology number two. "I made a mistake, Nate."

"About?"

"My conflict resolution lessons were all wrong. I thought the secret to resolving conflict was breathing to stay calm and pretending all was well no matter what. That isn't conflict resolution, it's conflict avoidance. I needed it to survive my childhood, but it doesn't work for couples."

"I agree."

This was going better than she'd hoped. "There's more," she said. "I shouldn't have broken up with you."

His shoulders sagged in relief. "That's good, because I want you back."

"Even after you saw me unglued?"

"I didn't like that you were mad at me, but I understood. You needed to let out your frustrations. Besides, you're beautiful when you're angry."

She choked out a laugh. "You don't have to go that far."

"I mean it. Don't ever hold back because of me. I won't, either. I want us to be upfront with each other. On that note, I promised to be open with you but I haven't been sharing my feelings. My parents never did, and I guess I learned from them. That changes now."

He picked up and gulped the coffee he'd

brought her, and she realized he was as on edge as she was.

"I love you," he said. "I have since the first time I saw you."

Becca didn't hide her disbelief.

"It's the truth. I figured I'd never have a chance with you and I moved on—or so I told myself. You've always been the woman I want and I don't see that ever changing."

Tears welled in her eyes. For the first time, she let Nate see them.

He seemed taken aback. "I said the wrong thing, huh? Please, don't cry. Just keep giving me those lessons. I'll improve."

"You're fine the way you are, Nate. These are happy tears. Funny, from the time Charlie introduced us all those years ago, I've had a secret crush on you. I didn't think you were interested so I pretended I wasn't, either. I still had that crush when we talked at Lucky Joe's. Before long, it grew into something deeper."

She smiled at this man she adored. "What I'm saying is, I love you, too. And I promise that from now on, I'll tell you right away when I'm upset or angry. No more holding back."

"You didn't hold back when this Charlie thing happened."

"Before that I did, only I hid it."

He frowned. "Really?"

He seemed genuinely curious and she wanted to tell him, even if doing so felt uncomfortable and risky. In time, she'd get used to it. "When we go out you never ask what I want to do or where I want to eat. You make the decision all by yourself. That bothers me."

"You've never chimed in. I figured you expected me to plan everything— a real chore. I'd rather know up front what you're thinking and what you want. Making you happy makes me happy. If it doesn't, I'll let you know. We have to trust each other enough to share stuff, no matter what."

Feeling like the luckiest woman alive, Becca smiled. "I like that, Nate. A lot. On that note..." She stood and held her hand out to him. "Here's what I want now—you. In my bed."

~

Two weeks later

As CHARLIE and Scarlett exchanged vows, Nate pinned his gaze on Becca. Standing a few yards away from him in a strapless dress that wowed him, she focused on the bride and groom. Sexy and beautiful, and all his. God above, he loved her.

Newly pronounced, husband and wife sealed their union with a kiss. Becca beamed at Nate, her eyes bright with joy and love for him, just as they would be when they exchanged their own vows.

Committed to each other through good and bad, facing together whatever challenges came their way.

Life didn't get any better than that.

THE END

THANK you for letting me share my stories with you!

IF YOU ENJOYED **MR. AUGUST**, help others find this book by recommending it to your friends and by writing a review. If you would like to know when my next release is available and other fun stuff, sign up for my newsletter here: www.an nroth.net

THERE ARE 12 sexy firefighter books planned for the **Heroes of Rogue Valley: Calendar Guys**

OTHER BOOKS:
   Halo Island:
   All I Want for Christmas

The Pilot's Woman
Ooh, Baby!

ANN ROTH CLASSICS:
Father of the Year
A Place to Belong
My Sisters
Another Life

VISIT ME AT FACEBOOK FACEBOOK.COM/ANN-ROTHAUTHORPAGE
Follow me onTwitter @Ann_Roth
Email me at ann@annroth.net
Visit my website www.annroth.net

THANKS, and until next time,
Ann

ALSO BY ANN ROTH

Halo Island

Book 1 All I Want for Christmas

Book 2 The Pilot's Woman

Book 3 Ooh, Baby!

Book 4 The One I Love

Miracle Falls

Book 1 Christmas in Miracle Falls

Book 2 Dream a Little Dream

Book 3 It Had to Be You

Book 4: You're the One That I Want

Saddlers Prairie

Book 1 Since I Fell for You

Book 2 I'll Be There

Book 3 Until There Was You